'You didn't say how old your son was.'

She felt the blood freeze in her veins, but she kept her face calm. 'That's because you didn't ask.'

'I'm asking now.'

A thousand thoughts began to make a scrambled journey through her mind. Could she carry it off? Would he see through the lie if she told him that Tim was four?

Her hesitation told him everything, as did the blanching of colour from her already pale face. 'He's mine, isn't he?'

She stared at him. 'Philip—'

'*Isn't* he?' he demanded, in a low harsh voice which cut through her like a knife.

She leant on the door for support, and nodded her head mutely.

'Say it, Lisi! Go on, *say* it!'

'Tim is your son,' she admitted tonelessly, and then almost recoiled from the look of naked fury in his eyes.

Sharon Kendrick started story-telling at the age of eleven and has never really stopped. She likes to write fast-paced, feel-good romances with heroes who are so sexy they'll make your toes curl!

Born in west London, she now lives in the beautiful city of Winchester—where she can see the cathedral from her window (but only if she stands on tiptoe). She is married to a medical professor—which may explain why her family get more colds than anyone else on the street—and they have two children, Celia and Patrick. Her passions include music, books, cooking and eating—and drifting off into wonderful daydreams while she works out new plots!

Recent titles by the same author:

THE UNLIKELY MISTRESS
SURRENDER TO THE SHEIKH
THE SICILIAN'S PASSION

THE MISTRESS'S CHILD

BY
SHARON KENDRICK

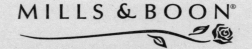

MILLS & BOON®

To the enigmatic Signor Candice.
And to the horse-riding Thomas Hietzker (Ave Maria).

*First published in Great Britain 2001
Harlequin Mills & Boon Limited,
Eton House, 18-24 Paradise Road, Richmond, Surrey TW9 1SR*

© Sharon Kendrick 2001

ISBN 0 263 82564 7

*Set in Times Roman 10½ on 11½ pt.
01-0102-51104*

*Printed and bound in Spain
by Litografía Rosés, S.A., Barcelona*

CHAPTER ONE

HE WALKED into the office and all her dreams and night-mares came true.

Lisi felt giddy. Sick. But maybe that was just the effect he was having on her heart-rate.

Up until that moment it had been a perfect day—her last afternoon at work before she finished for Christmas. There had been nothing bigger on her mind than the arrangements for Tim's birthday party the following day and wondering, along with everyone else, whether the threatened snow would fall.

She stared up into the cool, chiselled features and her fingers—which had been flying furiously over the key-board—froze into stillness. But so did the rest of her—heart, body and soul. For one long, timeless moment their eyes met and she wondered what on earth she could say to him, but just the sight of him was making speech impossible.

He was as devastating as he had always been, but his body looked leaner, harder—all tight, honed muscle which even the elegant winter coat couldn't disguise.

Instinct made her want to stand up and demand what he was doing there, to ask him how he had the nerve to show that heartbreaking face of his, but the stakes were much too high and she knew that she could not afford to give into instinct.

'Hello, Philip,' she said at last, astonished to hear how steady her voice sounded.

He should have been expecting it, but her effect on him took him completely off guard and the sound of her low,

5

husky voice ripped through his defences. Damn her, he thought bitterly as he recalled her soft white thighs wrapped around his body as he had plunged deep, deep inside her, unable to stop himself even though every fibre of his being had tried. Damn her!

He felt the leap of blood, like a fountain to his senses, and it felt like being resurrected. Months which had moved into years of living in an emotional and physical wasteland and she had vanquished his icy indifference simply by the lilting way she said his name. His normally lush, sensual mouth was thin and unsmiling.

'Why, for a moment there I thought you didn't remember me, Lisi,' he mocked softly.

Not remember him? She would have to be dead not to have remembered him, even if she hadn't had the living proof to remind her every single day of her life.

She kept her face impassive, but in reality she was greedily registering every detail of that arrogantly beautiful face. Thinking of her son's face and searching for heartbreaking signs of similarity—but thank God there was none. His lightly tanned golden skin was so very different from her son's natural pallor, as were Philip's startling emerald eyes. They made the aquamarine hue of Tim's look so diluted in comparison.

And then her heart began to race and the inside of her mouth turned to sandpaper as painful questions began to buzz silently around her head. Why was he here?

Did he *know?*

The foundations of her world threatened to rock on their axis, but she kept her face as calm as his. He couldn't know. He couldn't possibly know!

'Not remember you? Of course I remember you,' she said, in as bland a voice as she could manage—she even tacked on a weak attempt at a smile as she met the emerald ice of his stare. 'I always remember—'

'All the men you've slept with?' he challenged, unable to resist the taunt, cruelly pleased by the sting of colour which brought roses to the whiteness of her skin.

She felt heat flaring across her cheeks, but that was her only outward reaction to his remark. How blatant, to say something as provocative as that, she thought indignantly— especially when you considered *his* track record. And all the while looking at her with that cold, studied insolence which did nothing to mar the sheer beauty of his face.

She bit back the temptation to remind him that there had been no sleep involved. He had not wanted to sleep with her—and for very good reason. She repressed a shudder as she was reminded of what a gullible fool she had been.

Far better to change the subject completely. To find out what he wanted and to see the back of him.

'I was about to say that I always remember clients—' She wished that she could bite the word back. It seemed so cold and unfeeling in view of what she had shared, until she reminded herself that they had shared nothing—except their bodies.

'Clients,' she continued valiantly, 'who have involved this company in as many deals as you once did. You brought us a lot of business, Mr Caprice. We sold a lot of properties through you.'

So she remembered his surname, too. Philip didn't know whether to be flattered or not, though he was certainly surprised. He suspected that he had been just one in a long line of men she had enticed into her bed—a woman who looked like that would have no trouble doing so. Did she have a photographic memory for *all* their names?

He studied her—taking all the time in the world to do so—and why not? Hadn't she haunted his memory with bitter-sweet recall? Given him the acrid taste of guilt in his mouth every time he'd thought of her in nearly four years?

Even though he had tried his hardest not to think of her. Tried and failed every time.

But Lisi Vaughan had been a fever in his blood for far too long now.

His eyes skimmed over her. Time had not made much of a mark—certainly not on her face, which was probably the most beautiful he had ever seen. A face completely devoid of make-up, which gave it an odd kind of purity which seemed so at odds with her innate sensuality.

The eyes he remembered because they were icy and aquamarine—unique. Slanting, siren's eyes, half shielded by a forest of thick, dark eyelashes, which made her look so minxy. The darkness of her lashes was echoed in her hair—deep, dark ebony—as black as the coals of hell itself and made even blacker by its dramatic contrast to the whiteness of her skin. She looked like a witch, he thought, a beautiful temptress of a witch with a body which few men would see outside paradise.

He knitted his eyebrows together almost imperceptibly. Not that her body was on display much today, but some things you couldn't disguise—even though she had done her level best with some plain black skirt and high-necked blouse which made her look almost *dowdy*.

No. On second thoughts—certainly not dowdy. Philip swallowed as she moved her head back, as if trying to escape his scrutiny, and the movement drew attention to the unforgettable swell of her breasts. Her waist was as tiny as ever, but her breasts were slightly fuller, he thought, and then was punished with the heavy jackknifing of desire in response.

Lisi could feel her heartbeat growing thready and erratic. She wished he wouldn't look at her that way. It reminded her of too much she would rather forget. Of tangled limbs and the sheen of sweat, the sweet, fleeting pleasure of fulfilment followed by the shattering pain of rejection. He had no *right* to look at her that way.

She quashed down the desire to tell him to get out, and forced a pleasantry out instead. He was not the kind of man to be pushed. If she wanted him out of there—and she most certainly did—then he must come to the conclusion that it had been his idea to leave and not hers.

Keep it cool and keep it professional, she told herself. 'Now. How can I help you?'

He gave her a grim smile, not trusting himself to answer for a moment, and then he lifted his eyebrows in mocking question. 'What a sweetly expressed offer,' he murmured.

'Why, thank you,' she said demurely.

'Do you say that to all the men?'

'Most of them are grown-up enough not to read anything into it.' She matched his remark with a dry tone of her own and then fixed her eyes on his unwaveringly, trying not to be distracted by that dazzling green gaze. 'So. Are you interested in a property for sale, Mr Caprice?'

Her unemotional attitude was having precisely the wrong effect on him. 'Oh, what's with all this ''Mr'' stuff?' Again he felt the sting of life to his senses, but ruthlessly he subdued them and gave a short laugh instead. 'Come on, Lisi,' he purred. 'I think we can dispense with the formalities, don't you? Surely we are intimate enough with each other to use first names?'

'*Were* intimate,' she corrected, and the heat in her face intensified as she was forced to acknowledge it aloud. 'Past tense. Remember?'

How could he possibly forget? And wasn't that why he had come here today—to change the past back to present? To rid himself of her pervasive and unforgettable sensual legacy. Wouldn't a whole night lost in the scented curves of her siren's body mean that he would be free of the guilt and the longing for ever? Sensations which had somehow chained him to her, and made him unable to move on.

He looked around the office, where the Christmas decorations were glittering silver and gold. In the corner stood a small artificial tree which was decked with shining crimson-red baubles and tiny white fairy lights.

He found Christmas almost unbearable—he had forgotten its poignant lure while he had been away. You could tell yourself that it was corny. Commercial. That all its true values were forgotten these days—but it still got to you every time.

And this was his first Christmas back in England since working in Maraban, where of course they had not celebrated the feast at all. He had not even had to think about it.

He was slowly beginning to realise that living in the Middle East had protected him from all the things he did not want to think about. And Christmas brought with it all kinds of things he would rather not think about. Feelings, mostly. Feelings of remorse. The pain of loss and the pain of wanting. Or, rather, of not wanting. For too long now, his body had felt as unresponding as a block of ice until he had walked in here today and seen her, and now his groin was on fire with need. Damn her, he thought again. Damn her!

He gritted his teeth, his gaze moving to her hand. She wore no wedding ring, nor any pale sign that one might have been recently removed, either. But women these days lived with men at the drop of a hat and he needed to find out if she was involved with someone. But even if she *did* have another man—would that honestly prevent him from doing what he intended to do?

He sat down in the chair opposite her desk, spreading out his long legs and not missing the thinning of her mouth as she watched him do so. He coolly crossed one leg over

the other and felt a jerk of triumph as he saw her eyes
darken. She wants me, he thought and his heart thundered
in his chest. She still wants me.

'I must say that I'm surprised to see you still working
here,' he observed, looking around the office of the small
estate agency.

Lisi stiffened, warning herself not to get defensive. It was
none of his business. She owed him nothing, least of all
the truth.

'I just happen to like selling houses,' she said.

'I guess you do.' It had been another aspect of her character which he had been unable to fault—her unerring abil-
ity to match the right property to the right client. It had
been what had brought him back to this small English village time after time as he'd sought valuable property for a
clutch of wealthy buyers. In the beginning he had always
dealt with Jonathon, the owner and senior negotiator, but
after a while Lisi had taken over. Beautiful Lisi, with her
ready smile and soft, sympathetic manner.

Part of him had not expected to find her here. He had
imagined that she would be running her own place by
now—and it was more than a little disconcerting to see her
at the same desk, in the same office. As if time had stood
still, and she with it. He gave her a questioning look. 'Most
people would have moved on by now—to bigger and
brighter things.'

And leave her safety net? Her cushion?

Her job had been the one familiar constant in those dark,
far-off days when she had wondered just how she was going to cope—how could she ever have left it? 'Not me,'
she said staunchly.

'Why ever not?' he asked quietly, bemused—because
she had not only been good at her job, she had been am-
bitious, too.

She didn't break the gaze, even though her stomach was

churning over with anxiety, as if he somehow knew her secret and was just biding his time before he confronted her with it. Distract him, she thought. 'Why on earth should my job prospects interest you?'

'Call it curiosity,' he told her softly. 'Ex-lovers always interest me.'

Lisi repressed a shudder. She didn't feel like his ex-lover—she felt like a woman who had shared his bed under false pretences before he had disappeared dramatically from her life. But she didn't want to analyse *that*—not now and not with him here. Instead she took his question at face value.

'I love my job,' she said staunchly. 'It's convenient and it's local—and there's no reason why I should travel miles to find something which is already on my doorstep, is there?'

'I guess not.' But he couldn't help wondering why she had settled for such steady small-town life when she was still so young and beautiful. His eyes were drawn irresistibly to the lush lines of her mouth, knowing that he would never be satisfied until he got her out of his system one last time.

For good.

He gave a conventional smile as he forced himself to make conventional conversation. 'And of course Langley is a very pretty little village.'

Lisi was growing uncomfortable. She wished he would go. Just his proximity was making the little hairs on the back of her neck stand up like soldiers and she could feel the prickle of heat to her breasts. She remembered the lightning feel of his mouth as it caressed all the secret places of her body and thought how sad it was that no other man had ever supplanted him in her memory.

She cleared her throat. The last thing she wanted was to antagonise him and to arouse his suspicions, but she could not tolerate much more of him sitting across the desk from her while she remembered his love-making, the unmistakable glint in his eyes telling her that *he* was remembering, too.

'You still haven't told me how I can help you,' she asked quietly.

Philip narrowed his eyes. He didn't know what he had expected from her today. More anger, he guessed. Yes. Much more. And more indignation, too. Lisi looking down her beautiful nose at him for daring to reappear without warning and after so long. Particularly after the last words he had ever said to her.

Yet there was an unexpected wariness and a watchfulness about her rather than the out-and-out anger he might have expected, and he wondered what was the cause of it. Something was not as it should be.

He ran a long, reflective finger along the faint shadow which darkened his jaw. 'You mean am I here today on business? Or pleasure?'

She gave a thin smile. 'I hope it's the former! Because I don't think that the atmosphere between us could be described as pleasure—not by any stretch of the imagination.'

Oh, but how wrong she was! You didn't have to like a woman to want her. He knew that. Liking could die, but lust seemed to have a much longer shelf-life. 'Then maybe we should try and put that to rights.'

'By placing as much distance as possible between us, you mean?'

'Not exactly.' He leaned back in the chair and narrowed his eyes in provocative assessment. 'Why don't I take you for a drink after work instead?'

His audacity left her reeling, and yet there had been weeks and months when she had prayed for such a proposition, when she'd tried to tell herself that what had happened between them had all been one big misunderstanding and that there must be a perfectly reasonable explanation for his behaviour.

But those hopes had soon dwindled—along with the growing realisation that Philip Caprice had changed her life irrevocably. And how, she reminded herself. He had brought with him trouble and upheaval, and if she wasn't very, very careful—he could do the same all over again. And this time she had much more to lose.

'A drink? I don't think so. Not a very good idea,' she told him in a trembling voice and then paused for effect—to try and hurt him as much as he had once hurt her. 'I can't imagine that your wife would like it very much. Or has she grown used to your infidelities by now?'

He stilled as if she had struck him, though he had been expecting this accusation from the moment he'd walked in. He was surprised that she had taken so long to get around to it. 'My wife wouldn't know,' he said tonelessly.

'Oh, so it all became too much for her, did it?' Lisi sucked in a breath which threatened to choke her. 'Did she divorce you when she found out about me, Philip? Or were there others? There must have been, I guess—I'm not flattering myself that I was something special.'

He felt the pain of remorse. 'There was no divorce.' His eyes were very green—colder than ice and as unforgiving as flint. 'She—' He seemed to get ready to spit the next words out. 'She—died.'

Lisi registered the bizarre and unbelievable statement and flinched as she saw the brief bleakness which had flared up in his eyes.

Died? His wife had *died*? But how? And why? And when? Not that she could ask him. Not now. And just what could she say in a situation like this? Offer condolences for a woman she had unwittingly deceived? She swallowed down her awkwardness. 'I'm sorry—'

He shook his head. 'No, you're not. Don't pretend. You didn't know her.'

'Of course I didn't know her! I didn't even know *of* her, did I, Philip? Because if I had...if I had—' She chewed frantically on her lip.

'What?' he interjected softly. 'Are you trying to say that you wouldn't have gone to bed with me if you'd known she existed?'

'No,' she whispered. 'Of course I wouldn't.'

'Are you so sure, Lisi?'

She bent her head to gaze unseeingly at all the property details she had been typing up. Of course she wasn't sure. She wasn't sure of anything other than the fact that Philip Caprice had exercised some strange power over her—the power to transform her into the kind of wild, sensual creature she hardly recognised, and certainly didn't like.

'Just go away,' she said, her voice very low. 'Please, Philip. There's nothing left to say, and, even if there was, we can't have this conversation here.'

'I know we can't.' He leaned forward and the movement caused his trousers to ride and flatten over the strong, powerful shafts of his thighs and he heard her draw in a tiny breath. 'So let's have that drink later and catch up on old times. Aren't you interested to compare how the world has been treating us?'

Something in his words didn't ring true and again she felt a frisson of apprehension. Why would Philip suddenly reappear and want to *catch up on old times*?

'I don't think so.'

'Oh, come on, Lisi—what have you got to lose?'

Her freedom? Her sanity? Her *heart*? She shook her head. 'I'm busy after work,' she said, despising herself for being tempted all the same.

But there was something in her body language which told a conflicting story, something which put his senses on full alert—and, besides, he wasn't going away from here until he got what he had come for. 'How about tomorrow night then?'

'I'm busy.'

'You mean you have a date?'

Lisi stared at a face which held the arrogant expression of a man who was not used to being turned down, and came to a decision. She had thought that playing it polite might do the trick, that he might just take the hint and go away again. But she had been wrong. And the longer he stayed here…

Politeness abandoned now, she rose to her feet. 'I don't know how you have the cheek to ask that! My personal life is really none of your business, Philip.'

The fire in her eyes heated his blood, and there was answering fire from his as he echoed her movement and stood up to tower over her, thinking how small and how fragile she looked against his robust height.

'Like I said,' he murmured, 'I'm just curious about ex-lovers.'

Her heart was pounding with rage and fury and with something else, too—something far more threatening—something too closely linked with the overwhelming desire she had once felt for him. 'I don't think that the extent of our little *liaison* really warrants such a flattering description as ''ex-lover'', do you?'

He wasn't doing much thinking at all. Not now. He was entranced by the rise and fall of her heavy breasts beneath the thin white shirt and he felt an explosion of need and lust which made him grow exquisitely hard, and he thanked God that the heavy overcoat he wore concealed that fact.

'If the term offends, then what would you rather I called you, Lisi?' he asked steadily.

'I'd rather you didn't call me anything! In fact, I'd rather you turned straight around and went out the way you came in! What is the point of you being here? Do you honestly think you can just waltz back in here after all this time, and pick up where we left off?'

'Is that what you'd like, then?' he asked softly. 'To pick up where we left off?'

Yes! More than anything else in the world!

No! The very *last* thing she wanted!

Lisi stared distractedly at the hard, angular planes of his face and—not for the first time—wished that she had more than one beautiful yet unsatisfactory night to remember this man by. And then reminded herself that she had a whole lot more besides.

Imagine the repercussions if he were to find out!

She gave a humourless laugh. 'I outgrew my masochistic phase a long time ago!' She looked down deliberately at her watch. 'And now, if you'll excuse me, I really do have work to do!'

He remembered her as uncomplicated and easygoing, but now he heard the sound of unmistakable frost in her voice and he found himself overwhelmed by the urge to kiss the warmth back into it. And it was so long since he had felt the potency of pure desire that he found himself captive to his body's authority. Compelled to act by hunger and heat instead of reason—but then, that was nothing new, not with her.

A pulse began to beat at his temple. 'You don't look too busy to me.'

Like an onlooker in a play, Lisi stared with disbelief as she saw that he was moving around to her side of the desk, with a look on his face which told its own story.

'Philip?' she questioned hoarsely as he bent towards her.

'Answer me one thing and one thing only,' he demanded.

His voice was one of such stark command that Lisi heard herself framing the word, 'What?'

'Is there a man in your life?' he murmured. 'A husband or a fiancé or some long-time lover?'

This truth was easy to tell, but then perhaps that was because she was compelled to by the irresistible gleam of his eyes. She shook her head. 'No. No one.'

He looked down at her for one brief, hard moment and knew a moment of sheer, wild exultancy before he pulled her into his arms with a shudder as he felt the soft warmth of a woman in his arms again.

The blood roared in her ears. She wanted to push him away and yet she was powerless to move, so tantalising was his touch. Suddenly she knew just how a butterfly must feel shortly before it was impaled against a piece of card. Except that a butterfly would receive nothing but pain— while Philip could give her untold pleasure.

'What the hell do you think you're doing?' she breathed as she felt the delicious pressure of his fingers against her skin through the shirt she wore.

'You know what I'm doing.' Doing what he had been wanting to do ever since he had walked back in here again today. Doing what had haunted him for far too long now.

'You need kissing, Lisi,' he ground out and pulled her even closer. 'You know you do. You want me to. You always did. Didn't you?'

His arrogance took away what little of her breath was left, because just the sensation of feeling herself in the warm circle of his arms again was enough to make her feel as weak as a kitten.

'Get out of here! We're standing in the middle of my bloody *office*—' she spluttered, but her protest was cut short by the ringing of the doorbell and Marian Reece, her boss and the owner of Homefinders, walked in, her smile of welcome instantly replaced by one of slightly irritated bemusement as she took in the scene in front of her.

'Hello, Lisi,' she said steadily, looking from one to the other. 'I'm sorry—am I interrupting something?'

Hearing the unmistakable reproof in her boss's voice, Lisi sprang out of Philip's arms as if she had been scalded, thinking how close he had been to kissing her. Would she have let him? Surely not. But if she had...?

Her heart was crashing against her ribcage, but she struggled to retain her breath and to appear the kind of unflappable employee she usually was. 'H-hello, Marian. This is Philip Caprice. We were, um, we were just—'

'Just renewing our acquaintance,' interjected Philip smoothly and held his hand out to Marian, while smiling the kind of smile which few women would have the strength to resist.

And Marian Reece was not among them.

Lisi had known the forty-five-year-old since she had bought out the estate agency two years ago. She liked Marian, even though the older woman led a life which was streets apart from her own.

But then Marian was a successful businesswoman while Lisi was a struggling single mother.

'Lisi and I are old...friends,' said Philip deliberately. 'We go way back.'

'Indeed?' said Marian rather tightly. 'Well, call me a little old-fashioned—but mightn't this kind of fond greeting be better reserved for *out* of office hours?'

Fond? Inside, Lisi almost choked on the word. 'Yes, of course. And Philip was just leaving, weren't you, Philip?'

'Unfortunately, yes—I have some business to see to.' He glittered her a look which renewed the racing in her heart. 'But I'll be back tomorrow.'

Lisi thought it sounded more like a threat than a promise. 'Back?' she questioned weakly. 'Tomorrow?'

'Of course. You haven't forgotten that you're going to sell me a house, have you, Lisi?'

Lisi blinked at him in confusion. Had she had missed something along the way? 'A house?' He had mentioned *nothing* about a house!

'That's why I'm here,' he said gently. 'I'm looking for a weekend cottage—or something on those lines.'

Was she being offered a lifeline? In the old days he had done deals for rich contemporaries of his from university— they had valued his taste and his discretion.

'You mean you're buying for someone else?' Lisi stared up at him hopefully.

Her obvious resistance only increased his desire for her—although maybe she knew that. Maybe that was precisely why she was batting those aquamarine eyes at him like that and unconsciously thrusting the narrow curves of her hips forward. 'Sorry to disappoint you, sweetheart—but I'm looking for a country home for myself.'

Lisi's world threatened to explode in a cloud of black dust. 'Around *here*?' she questioned hoarsely.

'Sure. Why not? I know the area. It's very beautiful— and just about commutable from London.' His eyes mocked her. 'Sounds just about perfect to me.'

'Does it?' asked Lisi dully.

'Yes, of course we'll be delighted to find something for you, Mr Caprice,' said Marian crisply. 'I can look for you myself, if you prefer.'

He shook his head. 'Oh, no,' he contradicted softly. 'I'm quite happy to deal with Lisi.'

Well, I'm not happy to deal with *you*, she thought hysterically, but by then it was too late. He was charm personified to Marian as he said goodbye, and then he took Lisi's hand in his and held it for just a little longer than was necessary while he held her gaze.

'Goodbye, Lisi. Until tomorrow.'

'Goodbye, Philip.' She swallowed, while inside her heart raced with fear and foreboding.

She stood in silence with Marian as they watched him leave and Lisi's hands were shaking uncontrollably as the door clanged shut behind him.

Marian turned to look at her and her eyes were unexpectedly soft with sympathy. 'So when are you going to tell him, Lisi?' she asked softly.

Time froze. Lisi froze. 'Tell him what?'

'The truth, of course.' She placed a perfectly manicured hand on Lisi's shaking arm. 'He's the father of your child, isn't he?'

CHAPTER TWO

LISI stared at Marian. 'You can't know that!' she babbled, and now her knees really *were* threatening to give way. 'Tim looks nothing like him!'

'Sit down, dear, before you fall down.' Marian gently pushed her back down onto her chair and went and poured a glass of water from the cooler, then handed it to her. 'Now drink this—you've gone even paler than usual.'

Lisi sucked the chilled liquid into her parched mouth and then shakily manoeuvred it to a corner of her desk before raising her eyes beseechingly to her boss. 'He doesn't look anything like Philip,' she repeated stubbornly.

'Lisi,' said Marian patiently. 'Tim is your living image— but that doesn't mean that he hasn't inherited any of his father's characteristics. Sometimes a mother can blind herself to what she doesn't want to see. Sometimes it's easier for an outsider to see the true picture. I knew immediately that Philip was Tim's father.'

'But how?' Lisi demanded brokenly.

Marian sighed. 'Well, Tim is an unusually tall boy for his age—we've always said that. He has his father's strength and stature—and there's a certain look of him in the shape of his face, too.'

A chasm of frightening dimensions was beginning to open up in front of Lisi's feet. 'A-anything else?' she demanded hoarsely.

Marian shrugged awkwardly. 'Well, I've never seen you behave like that with a man before—'

'Because he was hugging me in the office, you mean?'

'*Hugging* you?' Marian raised her eyes to heaven.

22

'That's a new way to describe it! He looked more like he wanted to eat you up for breakfast, lunch and tea—and vice versa. Like no one else existed in the universe other than him.'

And he had always had that effect on her—even though she could have been nominated for an Oscar, so hard had she always tried to hide it in the past. Philip could do and behave exactly as he pleased and Lisi would always be there with a smile for him. No questions, Lisi. Weak Lisi. Foolish Lisi.

Well, not any longer!

'It must have been a very passionate relationship,' observed Marian.

If only she knew!

'The question is, what are you going to tell him?'

Lisi shook her head. 'I'm not. I'm not going to tell him.'

Marian screwed her eyes up. 'Oh, Lisi—do you honestly think that's a good idea?'

Lisi shook her head. 'I know it isn't ideal, but it's the only thing I can do.'

'But why, dear? Why not tell him? Don't you think he has the right to know that he has a beautiful son?'

'The right?' Lisi looked at her boss and knew that she could not tell her whole story—but part of the story would surely make her point for her. And illustrate as well as anything just how little she had meant to Philip.

'Marian—he walked out on me. He made it clear that he thought our night together was a big mistake, and that he wanted nothing more to do with me.'

Marian frowned. 'One night? That's all it was? Just one night?'

Lisi nodded. 'That's right.' She saw Marian's rather shocked face. 'Oh, it wasn't the *classic* one-night stand— believe me.' It hadn't even been meant to happen. 'I...I used to see him every couple of months or so,' she continued painfully. 'We had grown to like one another, though I realise now that I never really knew him, or anything about him. But the ''affair'' wasn't really an affair, as such.' In fact, it hadn't lasted beyond midnight.

'But isn't it time he found out the truth—whatever has happened between you? I have children of my own, Lisi, and children *need* a father wherever possible. They need to know their roots and where they come from.'

Lisi sighed. How could she possibly explain this without sounding scheming and cold-hearted? 'Maybe I'll tell him if he shows any sign of wanting to *be* a father, but if I just announce it without careful consideration—can't you just imagine the consequences? Philip demanding contact. Philip turning up to take Tim out...' Philip taking Tim's affection...while feeling nothing for her but lust at best, and contempt at worst. 'Tim doesn't even *know* about Philip!'

'But surely other people round here must know he's the father? *Someone* must know?'

Lisi shook her head. Her night with Philip had gone unnoticed and unremarked upon, and that was how she had kept it. No one knew the truth except for her mother, and that had been a death-bed secret. Even her best friend Rachel thought that her refusal to divulge the identity of Tim's father was down to some fierce kind of pride at having been deserted, but it went much deeper than that.

Lisi had accepted that Philip could and had just walked out of *her* life—but she had vowed that he would never play emotional ping-pong with that of her son. A child was a commitment you made for life, not something to be picked up and put down at will—especially if the father of that child was married.

Except now that his wife was dead. So didn't that change things?

Lisi shook her head. 'Nobody knows. Not a living soul.' She stared at Marian. 'Except for you, of course.'

'I won't tell him, if that's what you're worried about, Lisi,' said Marian awkwardly. 'But what if he finds out anyway?'

'He can't! He won't!'

'He's planning on buying a house here. It's a small village. What if he starts putting two and two together and coming up with the right answer? Surely he'll be able to work out for himself that he's the father?'

Lisi shook her head. Why should he? It was a long time ago. Months blurred into years and women blurred into other women, until each was indistinguishable from the last. 'Maybe he won't find a house to suit him?' she suggested optimistically, but Marian shook her head with a steely determination which Lisi recognised as the nine-carat businesswoman inside her.

'Oh, no, Lisi—don't even think of going down that road. This is strictly business. And if a client—any client—wants to buy a house from this agency, then we find one for him to buy. Beginning and end of story. I simply can't allow you to prejudice any sale because of some past quarrel with your child's father—which in my opinion, needs some kind of resolution before Tim gets much older.'

'An outsider doesn't know how it feels,' said Lisi miserably.

'Maybe that's best. An outsider can tell you what she thinks you *need* rather than what you think you *want*.' Marian's face softened again. 'Listen, dear,' she said gently, 'why don't you take the rest of the afternoon off? You look much too shaken to do any more work. Peter will be back from his viewing shortly—and it's always quiet at this time of the year. Think about what I've said. Sleep on it. It may be better in the long run if you just come clean and tell Philip the truth about Tim.'

Better for whom? wondered Lisi as she took off her work shoes and changed into the wellington boots she always wore to work when the weather was as inclement as it was today. It certainly wouldn't be better for *her*.

She felt disorientated and at a loss, and not just because of Philip's unexpected reappearance. Tim didn't finish nursery until four, which meant that she had nearly two hours going spare and now she wasn't quite sure what to do with them. How ironic. All the times when she had longed for a little space on her own, when the merry-go-round of work and single motherhood had threatened to drag her down—and here she was with time on her hands and wishing that she had something to fill it.

She didn't want to go home, because if she did then she would feel guilty for not putting any washing into the machine, or preparing supper for Tim, or any of the other eight million tasks which always needed to be done. And mundane tasks would free up her mind, forcing her to confront the disturbing thoughts which were buzzing around inside her head.

Instead, she turned up her coat collar against the chill breeze, and headed up the main village street, past the duck pond.

The light was already beginning to die from the sky and the contrasting brightness of the fairy lights and glittering Christmas trees which decorated every shop window made the place look like an old-fashioned picture postcard. How their gaiety mocked her.

The breeze stung her cheeks, and now and again, tiny little flakes of snow fluttered down from the sky to melt on her face like icy tears.

The weathermen had been promising a white Christmas, and, up until today, it had been one of Lisi's main preoccupations—whether her son would see his first snow at the most special time of year for a child.

But thoughts of a white Christmas had been eclipsed by thoughts of Philip, and now they were threatening to engulf her, making her realise just why she had put him in a slot in her memory-bank marked 'Closed'. She had done that for reasons of practicality and preservation—but seeing him today had made it easy to remember just why no one had ever come close to replacing him in her affections.

And now he might be here to stay.

She climbed over a stile and slid down onto wet grass, glad for the protection of her heavy boots as she set out over the field, but she had not walked more than a few metres before she realised that she was being followed.

Lisi knew the village like the back of her hand. She had lived there all her life and had never felt a moment's fear or apprehension.

But she did now.

Yet it was not the heartstopping and random fear that a stranger had materialised out of nowhere and might be about to pounce on her, because some sixth sense warned her to the fact that the person following her was no stranger. She could almost sense the presence of the man who was behind her.

She stopped dead in her tracks and slowly turned around to find Philip standing there, his unsmiling face shadowed in the fast-fading light of dusk. Out here in the open countryside he seemed even more formidable, his powerful frame silhouetted so darkly against the pale apricot of the sky, and Lisi felt the sudden warm rush of desire.

And she didn't want to! Not with him. Not with this beautiful, secretive and ultimately deceitful man who had given her a child and yet would never be a father to that child.

She had overplayed the bland, polite card in the office today and he had not taken heed of her wish to be rid of him. The time for politeness was now past.

'Do you always go creeping up on people in the twilight, Philip?' she accused.

He gave a faint smile. 'Sometimes. My last employment meant that I had to employ qualities of stealth, even cunning.'

She resisted the urge to suggest that the latter quality would come easily to him, intrigued to learn of what he had been doing for the past four years. 'And what kind of employment was that?'

He didn't answer immediately. He wasn't sure how much of his past he wanted to share with her. What if anything he wanted to share with her, other than the very obvious. And his years as emissary to a Middle Eastern prince could not be explained in a couple of sentences in the middle of a field on a blisteringly cold winter's afternoon. 'Maybe I'll tell you about it some time,' he said softly.

So he wasn't going to fill in any gaps. He would remain as unknowable as he ever had been. She looked at him in exasperation. 'Why are you really here, Philip? What brought you back to Langley after so long?'

An unanswerable question. How could he possibly define what his intentions had been, when nothing was ever as easy as you thought it was going to be? *Something* had compelled him to return and lay a increasingly troublesome ghost to rest, and yet the reality was proving far more complex than that.

He had been dreaming of her lately. Images which had come out of nowhere to invade his troubled nights. Not pin-point, sharply accurate and erotic dreams of a body which had captivated him and kept him prisoner all this time. No, the dreams had been more about the elusive memory of some far-distant sweetness he had experienced in her arms.

Part of him had wondered if seeing her again would make the hunger left by the dream disappear without trace—like the pricking of a bubble with a pin—but it had not happened like that.

The other suspicion he had nurtured—that her beauty and charm would be as freshly intact as before—had sprung into blinding and glorious Technicolor instead. His desire for her burned just as strongly as before—maybe even more so—because nobody since Lisi had managed to tempt him away from his guilt and into their bed.

Not that there hadn't been offers, of course, or invitations—some subtle, some not. There had been many—particularly when he had been working for the prince—and some of those only a fool would have turned down. Was that what he was, then—a fool?

Or was it that one night with her had simply not been enough? Like a starving man only being offered a morsel when the table was tempting him with a banquet?

He looked into her eyes—their bright, clear aquamarine shaded a deeper blue by the half-light of approaching dusk. Her face was still pale—pale as the first faint crescent of the moon which was beginning its nightly rise into the heavens. Her lips looked darker, too. Mulberry-coloured—berry-sweet and succulent and juicy—what wouldn't he give to possess those lips again?

'Maybe I wanted to see you again,' he murmured.

It sounded too much like the kind of declaration which a woman dreamed a man would make to her, but there was no corresponding gentling of his tone when he said it. The deep-timbred voice gave as little away as the green, shuttered eyes did.

'Why?' She forced herself to say it. 'To sleep with me again?'

Philip's mouth hardened. He wasn't going to lie. 'I think you know the answer to that.'

She let out a cold, painful breath as the last of her hopes crumbled. It was as she had suspected. The warm, giving

Philip whose bed she had shared—that man did not exist. It had all been an act. He was merely a seductive but illusionary figure who had let his defences down enough to have sex with her, and then had retreated to his real world—a world which had excluded her because he'd had a wife.

Not just cruel, but arrogant, too!

'And you think…' She sucked in a deep breath. 'Do you really think that I've been sitting around, just waiting for you to come back and make such a—' she almost choked on the word '—*charming* declaration as that one?'

'But I'm not telling you any lies, am I, Lisi?'

She shook her head violently, and some of the thick, dark hair escaped from the velvet ribbon which had held it captive. 'No,' she agreed. 'Lies aren't your thing, are they? You lie by omission rather than fact! Like you omitted to tell me that you were married when you seduced me!'

'*Seduced* you?' He gave a short laugh and his breath clouded the air like smoke. 'You make it sound as though we were both starring in some kind of Victorian melodrama! There was no wicked master seducing some sweet little innocent who knew no better, was there, Lisi? Quite the contrary, in fact. You were the one who stripped naked in my bed. You knew exactly what you wanted and what you were doing. So please don't play the innocent. That night you kept me delightfully and memorably entertained—something which is simply not compatible with someone who isn't…' he narrowed his eyes into hard, condemnatory slits '…*experienced.*'

Lisi swallowed. He was insulting her, she knew that—and yet it was like no insult she had ever heard. The disparaging tone which had deepened his voice did not have her itching to slap the palm of her hand against that smooth, golden cheek the way it should have done.

Instead, it seemed to have set off a chain reaction which

began with the quickened pace of her heart and ended with the honey-slick throb of a longing so pure and so overwhelming that she could have sunk down into the thick, wet clods of earth and held her arms open to him.

But she had played the fool with Philip Caprice once before, and once was too often.

She raised her eyebrows. 'You know, you really ought to make your mind up how you feel about me. On the one hand you seem to despise me for my so-called experience—while on the other you seem unable to forget what happened.'

'Can you?' he demanded as he felt the heavy pull of need deep in his groin. 'Can you forget it, Lisi?'

Of course she couldn't! But then, unlike Philip, she had a very tangible memory of that night.

Tim.

She thought of Marian's words—wise, kindly experienced Marian who had urged her to tell him, who had emphasised how much a child needed a father. But what if this particular man had no desire to be a father? What if she told him and ruined both her and Tim's lives unnecessarily? What if Philip had *children of his own*?

Was now the time to ask him? In a field on a cold December night where stars were now beginning to appear as faint blurry dots in the skies?

She steeled herself. 'What happened to your wife, Philip?'

She took him off guard with her question, though perhaps that was because these days he had schooled himself not to remember Carla more than was absolutely necessary. The living had to let go—he knew that—just as he knew how hard it could be.

He used the same words as the press had done at the time. 'She was involved in a pile-up on the motorway.'

She nodded, painfully aware of how much the bereaved

resented other people's silence on the subject. She remembered when her mother had died, and people had seemed to cross the road to avoid her. 'Was it...was it instant?'

'*No.*' The word came out more harshly than he had intended, but he did not want to discuss Carla, not now. God forgive him, but he wanted to lose the pain of death in the sweet, soft folds of living flesh. 'Can't we go somewhere warmer, if we're going to talk?'

She shook her head. Tim would be out of nursery soon enough and she had no desire to take Philip home and have him see her little house with all its childish paraphernalia, which might just alert his suspicions.

And where else to go to talk in Langley on one of the shortest days of the year—the pub would have shut by now. There was always the hotel, of course, she reminded herself, and a shiver of memory ran down her spine.

'I don't think there's any point in talking. What is there left to say?'

He watched the movement of her lips as she spoke, saw the tiny moist tip of her tongue as it briefly eased its way between her perfect white teeth, and a wave of lust turned his mouth to dust. 'Maybe you're right,' he agreed softly. 'How can we possibly talk when this crazy attraction is always going to be between us? You still want me, Lisi— it's written all over your face,' and he reached out and pulled her into his arms.

'D-don't,' she protested, but it was a weak and meaningless entreaty and she might as well not have spoken for all the notice he took of it.

He cupped her face in the palm of his hand and turned it up so that she was looking at him, all eyes and lips and pale skin, and his voice grew soft, just as once it had before. 'Why, you're cold, Lisi,' he murmured.

It was the concern which lulled her into staying in his arms—that and the masculine heat and the musky, virile scent of him. Helplessly, she stared up at him, knowing that he was about to kiss her, even before he began to lower his mouth towards hers.

The first warm touch of him was like clicking on a switch marked 'Responsive'. 'Philip,' she moaned softly, without realising that she was doing so, nor that her arms had snaked up around his neck to capture him.

The way she said his name incited him, and he whispered hers back as if it were some kind of incantation. 'Lisi.' Her mouth was a honey-trap—warm and soft and immeasurably sweet. He felt the moistness of her tongue and the halting quality of her breath as it mingled with his. Even through the thickness of his greatcoat, he could feel the flowering of her breasts as they jutted against him and he felt consumed with the need to feel them naked once more, next to his body and tickling both hard and soft against his chest. 'Oh, Lisi,' he groaned.

All she could think of was that this was not just the man she had found more overwhelmingly attractive than any other man she had ever met—this man was also the biological father of her child, and in a way she was chained to him for ever.

Just for a minute she could pretend that they had been like any other couple who had created a child together. They could kiss in a field and she could lace her fingers luxuriously through the thick abundance of his hair, and feel the quickening of his body against hers and then…and then…

Then what?

The logical conclusion to what they were starting clamoured into her consciousness like a bucket of ice-cold water being torrented over her and Lisi pulled herself out of his arms, her eyes wide and darkened, her breath coming in short, laboured little gasps.

'You thought it would be that simple, did you, Philip? One kiss and I would capitulate?'

The ache of her absence made his words cruel. He raised his eyebrows in laconic mockery. 'You weren't a million miles away from capitulation, were you?'

She drew her coat around her tightly and the reality of the winter afternoon made her aware that she was chilled almost to the bone. 'I may have had a moment's weakness,' she hissed, 'but I can assure you that I have, or *had*, absolutely no intention of letting you take me in some damp and desolate field as if I were just some girl you'd picked up at a party and thought you'd try your luck with!'

'Luck?' he said bleakly, stung by the irony of the word. Maybe it was time he told her. Maybe he owed her that much. For what kind of bastard could have walked out on a woman like Lisi with only the baldest of explanations— designed not just to hurt her but to expurgate his own guilt? 'I really do think we need to have that talk, Lisi—but not now, and not here—'

'I don't think talking is what you *really* have in mind, do you?' she enquired archly. 'So please don't dress up something as simple as longing by trying to give it a respectable name!'

'Something as simple as longing?' he echoed wryly. 'You think that longing is ever in any way simple?'

'It can be for some people!' she declared hotly. 'Boy meets girl! Boy falls in love with girl!'

'Boy and girl live happily ever after?' he questioned sardonically. 'I'm a little too old to believe in fairy tales any more, Lisi, aren't you?'

His scent was still like sweet perfume which clung to her skin, and she drew away from him, frightened by the depth of how much she still wanted him. 'I'm going home now,' she said shakily, and fought down the desire to do the impossible. 'And I'm not taking you with me.'

He nodded, seeing that she was fighting some kind of inner battle, perversely pleased that she was not going to give into what he was certain she wanted. Maybe it had all happened too quickly last time. Maybe this time he should take it real slow. 'I'll walk with you.'

Her heart missed a beat. 'No, you won't!' She didn't want him to see where she lived, or catch a glimpse of her as she left the tiny cottage to go and collect Tim. And then what? For him to observe the angel-child who was her son and to start using that clever mind of his to work out that Tim was *his* son as well?

It was too enormous a decision to make on too little information, and who knew what Philip Caprice really wanted, and why he was here? She wasn't going to take the chance. Not yet.

'I'm not letting you walk home alone,' he said imperturbably.

Was it her imagination, or had he grown more than a little *autocratic* in the intervening years? 'Philip—this is the twenty-first century, for goodness' sake! How do you think I've managed to get by all these years, without you leaping out of the shadows ready and willing to play the Knight in Shining Armour? Langley is safe enough for a woman to walk home alone—why else do you think I've stayed here this long?'

He gave her a steady look. 'I don't know, Lisi. That's what makes it so perplexing. It doesn't add up at all.'

Her breath caught like dust in her throat. 'Wh-what doesn't?'

'You. Sitting like Miss Havisham at the same desk in the same office in the same estate agency. What kind of a life is that? What's your game plan, Lisi—are you going to stay there until you're old and grey and let life and men just pass you by?'

She caught a sudden vivid image of herself painted by

his wounding words. A little old woman, stooped and bent—her long hair grown grey, her skin mottled and tired from the day-in, day-out struggle of being a single mother, where money was tight. And Tim long gone. She drew in a deep sigh which was much too close to a sob, but she held the sob at bay.

'I don't have to stay here and be insulted by you,' she told him quietly. 'Why don't you just go away, Philip? Go back to where you came from and leave me alone!'

He gave a wry smile. If only it were as easy as that. He didn't try to stop her as she turned away from him and ran back over the field, the heavy mud and the heavy boots making her progress slow and cumbersome.

But she leapt over the stile like a gazelle and he stood watching the last sight of her—her hair almost completely free of its confinement now, and it danced like crazy black snakes which gleamed in the light of the moon—while his heart pounded like a piston in his chest.

CHAPTER THREE

LISI ran and ran without turning back, as if he were chasing her heels—and wasn't there part of her which wished that he were?

But once she was safely out onto the village street and she realised that Philip was not intent on pursuing her, she slowed her pace down to a fast walk. She didn't want to alarm anyone by looking as though the hounds of hell were snapping at her heels.

Her cottage was tucked up a little incline, three streets away from the shops, and she fumbled her key into the brightly painted blue front door, closing it firmly behind her, safe at last.

The place was small, but it was cosy and it was home and it suited the two of them just fine. Lisi had bought it once her mother's big house had been sold—a big, rambling old place which would have cost a fortune to run and maintain.

She drew the curtains and went round the room switching on the lamps and creating a warm, homely glow. Later, once she had collected Tim, she would light the fire and they would toast crumpets and play together—her son completely oblivious of the knowledge of whom she had just seen.

While down in the village his father would spend the evening doing God only knew what while she kept her momentous secret to herself.

Lisi shook her head. She felt like pouring herself a large drink and then another, but she wasn't going to start doing *that*. Instead she put on an extra sweater and made herself a cup of tea, then curled up on the sofa with her fingers curled around the steaming mug.

She looked at Tim's advent calendar which hung next to the fireplace. Only seven days lay unopened. Seven days until Christmas and only one until his birthday tomorrow.

Had fate made Philip turn up at the time of such a milestone in Tim's life? Or a cruel and bitter irony?

She remembered the birth as difficult—partly because she had gone through it all on her own. Lisi's fingers tightened around the mug. Just thinking about the long and painful labour cut through her carefully built defences, and the memories of Philip which she had kept at bay for so long came flooding out, as if her mind had just burst its banks, like a river.

It had started innocently enough—though afterwards she thought about whether there was ever complete innocence between a man and a woman. When and how did simple friendship become transmuted into lust?

The first few times he saw her he completely ignored her, his cool green eyes flicking over her with a disappointing lack of interest.

She knew exactly who he was, of course—everyone in the office did. Rich, clever, enigmatic Philip Caprice who owned a huge estate agency in North London.

He was something of a scout, too—because people seeking discretion and a home in the country flocked to him to find them the perfect place. Rich—fabulously rich—clients who had no desire for the world and his wife to know which property they were in the process of buying. According to Jonathon, he handled house sales for film stars and moguls and just plain old-fashioned aristocracy.

He always dealt with Jonathon. In fact, Lisi was the office junior, only six months into the job, and eager to learn. Jonathon had let her handle a couple of accounts—but terraced cottages and houses on the new estate on the outskirts of Langley were not in Philip Caprice's league!

And then he walked in one lunchtime, on the day after her twenty-second birthday. She had been left on her own in the office for the first time. Jonathon was at lunch and Saul Miller, her other colleague, was out valuing a property which was coming onto the market shortly.

The phones were quiet and all her work up to date and Lisi felt contented with life. She was wearing her birthday sweater—a dream of a garment in soft blue cashmere which her mother had bought—and her hair was tied back in a ribbon of exactly the same shade.

On her desk were the remains of her birthday cake and she was just wondering whether to throw it away or stick a piece of cling-film round it and put it in the fridge. Jonathon seemed to have hollow legs, and it *did* seem a shame to waste it.

The door to the office clanged and in came Philip and her heart gave its customary leap. His hair was thick and nut-brown, ruffled by the breeze, and he wore an exquisitely cut suit which immediately marked him out as a Londoner.

For a moment, words deserted her. He seemed to dwarf the room with his presence—it was a little like having a Hollywood film star walk into a small-town estate agency!

She swallowed. 'Good morning, Mr Caprice.'

He gave a curt nod. 'Jonathon not around?'

'He's not back yet. He, er—' she glanced down nervously at her watch, and then lifted her eyes to him '—he shouldn't be long. You're—er—you're a bit earlier than expected.'

'The roads were clear,' he said shortly. 'I'll wait. No problem.'

He didn't look as though he meant it and Lisi thought that his face looked bleak, as if he had had a long, hard morning—no, make that a long, hard month. There was a restless, edgy quality about him, as if he hadn't slept properly for a long time. She said the first, impulsive thing which came into her head and pointed to her desk. 'Would you like some birthday cake?'

He narrowed his eyes as if she had just offered him something vaguely obscene. 'Birthday cake?' He frowned. 'Whose? Yours?'

Lisi nodded. 'That's right. It's really quite nice—a bit sickly, perhaps, but birthday cakes *should* be sickly, I always think, don't you?' She was aware that she was babbling but something in the slightly askance question in his eyes made her babble on. 'Won't you have some?'

There was something sweet and guileless about her eager chatter which completely disarmed him. Nor was he completely oblivious to the slenderly curved figure and the white skin and black hair which made her look like some kind of home-spun Snow White. But with the ease of practice he dismissed her physical attractions and stared at the cake instead.

Lisi could see him wavering. She remembered how much her father had loved cake when he'd been alive. What did her mother always say? 'Show me a man who says he doesn't like cake, and I'll show you a liar!'

'Oh, go on!' she urged softly. 'Have some—I was only going to throw it away!'

'Now there's an offer I can't refuse!' He laughed, and he realised how alien his own laughter sounded to his ears. When had he last laughed so uninhibitedly? He couldn't remember. 'Sure,' he said, because he hadn't eaten much since yesterday. 'Why not?'

She was aware of his green eyes on her as she cut him a hefty portion and piled it onto one of the paper plates she had brought in with her. 'The last of Minnie Mouse.' She smiled, as she handed it to him. 'See? You've got her spotty skirt!'

'So I see,' he murmured. 'Aren't you a little old for Minnie Mouse?'

'Twenty-two,' she said, in answer to a question he hadn't asked, and when he frowned rather repressively she added inconsequentially, 'I *love* Disney characters—I always have!'

He took the plate from her and sat down in the chair opposite her desk, and bit into the cake. She had been right. Too sweet. Too sickly. Bloody delicious. He tried and failed to remember the last time he had eaten birthday cake. Or celebrated a birthday. Or celebrated anything. But there hadn't been a whole lot to celebrate lately, had there?

Lisi watched him, pleased to see him eating it with such obvious appetite. She thought how fined-down his face seemed, and wondered when was the last time he had eaten properly. She struggled against the instinct to offer to take him home and to have her mother cook a decent meal of meat and two veg with a vast portion of apple pie afterwards.

What was she *thinking* of? The man was a client! And a very well-heeled client, too—not the kind of man who would thank her for trying to mother him!

She licked her lips unconsciously as she looked at his long fingers breaking off another piece. Maybe mothering was the wrong word to use. There were probably a lot more satisfying things a woman would feel like doing to Philip Caprice than mothering, she realised, shocked by her wayward thoughts.

She watched him finish every crumb on his plate and decided to show him how efficient she could be. 'Right then, Mr Caprice—let me find these properties for you to have a look at—Jonathon has sorted them all out for you.'

She bent her head as she began flicking through an old-fashioned filing box, and Philip felt an uncomfortable and unwanted fluttering of awareness as he looked at the ebony sheen of her hair and the long, elegant line of her neck.

Out of necessity, he had schooled himself not to be tempted by women, and certainly not women who were such a devastating combination of the innocent and the sensual, but for once he felt his resolve waver.

'Here we are.' Lisi found the last of what she was looking for, and held them out to him.

He noticed the way that the tip of her tongue protruded from between her teeth when she was concentrating. Tiny and pink. Shiny. He swallowed. 'Thanks.' He leaned across the desk and took the sheaf of house details from her.

'Jonathon should be back any minute, unless—' she gave him her most hopeful smile '—you'd like *me* to show you round?' She would have to leave the office unattended for a while, but Jonathon would be back from lunch any minute. She saw him frown and hoped that hadn't sounded like some sort of come-on. She blushed. 'I know I'm relatively inexperienced, but I'd be more than happy to.'

She seemed sweet and uncomplicated, and he couldn't deny that he wasn't tempted, but he steeled his heart against temptation.

'Listen, Jonathon knows me pretty well. He knows the kind of thing I like.' He saw her face fall, as if he'd struck her a blow, and he felt the sweet remains of the birthday cake in his mouth and sighed. 'Maybe next time, perhaps?'

This cheered Lisi up considerably, and later, when Jonathon had come back from the viewings and Philip had gone, she began to quiz him in a very casual way.

'He seems nice,' she offered.

Jonathon was busy writing up the offer which Philip Caprice had just made on some sprawling mid-Victorian mansion. 'Nice? Huh! Ruthless would be a better description! He's just got himself a terrific property at a knock-down price—beats me how he does it!'

'Maybe he's just a good businessman?' suggested Lisi serenely.

Jonathon scowled. 'Meaning I'm not, I suppose?'

'No, of course not—that wasn't what I meant at all!' Lisi glanced over his shoulder. 'Anyway—that isn't far off the asking price, is it?'

'True.' Jonathon sighed. 'If only he hadn't managed to wheedle out of the owner that they were desperate for a quick sale we might have held out for the full price.'

'I thought we were supposed to tell the vendor to keep out of negotiations with the purchaser, wherever possible?'

'I did,' said Jonathon glumly, then added, 'Only it was a *woman*. She took one look at him and decided to give him a gushingly guided tour of the place—only unfortunately it backfired. After that, he had her eating out of his hand and she's several thousand pounds out of pocket as a result.'

So was that ruthless, or just good business-sense? Whatever it was, it wasn't really surprising—Lisi thought that he could probably have *any* woman eating out of his hand.

'What's he like?' she asked. 'As a person?'

'Who knows?' Jonathon shrugged. 'He keeps his cards very close to his chest. I've dealt with him on and off for ages and I know next to nothing about him—'

Other than the very obvious attributes of being rich and gorgeous and irresistible to women, thought Lisi and put him out of her mind.

Until next time he came in.

Jonathon had gone to do some photocopying in the back room, and Lisi looked up to see the strikingly tall figure standing in the doorway and her heart gave a queer lurch. She frowned, shocked by the deep lines of strain which were etched onto his face.

Now there, she thought, is a man who is driving himself much too hard.

Philip glanced across the room to see the Birthday Girl sitting at her desk and smiling at him, and realised that he didn't even know her name.

'Hello, Mr Caprice!' she said cheerfully.

Reluctantly he smiled back—but there was something about her which made him *want* to smile. 'I think the trade-off for your delicious cake was that we should be on first-name terms, don't you? Except that I don't know yours.'

'It's Lisi—short for Elisabeth. Lisi Vaughan.'

Pretty name, he thought, and the question seemed to come out of nowhere. 'So are you going to show me around today, Lisi Vaughan?'

Lisi gulped, her heart banging excitedly in her chest. 'Are you sure you want me to?'

'Only if you're confident you can.'

She knew that confidence was the name of the game—particularly in selling—and why on earth should her confidence desert her just because she was about to accompany the most delicious man she had ever seen? She gave him her most assured smile. 'Oh, yes. I'm confident! That's if Jonathon doesn't mind.'

'I'll make sure he doesn't,' he said easily.

Jonathon knew better than to argue with his most prestigious client. 'Sure,' he agreed. 'Let's throw her in at the deep end!'

The viewing was unsuccessful—at least from a buying point of view. Philip tore the places to pieces in his car as he drove her back to the office afterwards.

'Overpriced!' he scorned. 'I don't know how people can ask that much—not when you consider how run-down the property is! And when you look what they've done to the garden—that garage they've built is nothing short of monstrous!'

'You didn't like it, then?' asked Lisi meekly.

He swiftly turned his head and, seeing her expression, laughed. 'Oh, very perceptive,' he murmured sardonically. 'You were good, Lisi,' he added unexpectedly.

'Was I?'

'Very good.' She had diplomatically left the monstrous garage until last and drawn his attention to all the good points in the house, but not in an in-your-face kind of way. She was chatty, but not intrusive, beautiful yet not flirtatious. In other words, she was a little like a glass of water—refreshing, but without any pernicious undertaste.

He sighed. Most of the women he met these days were nurses, and then only in a grimly professional capacity. Not that he wanted to meet women, of course he didn't—not with Carla lying so...so...

He flinched and changed gear more aggressively than he had intended to.

'It's a shame there's nothing else you're interested in,' Lisi was saying. 'I'll keep an eye out for your dream house!'

He threw her a rather mocking look. 'Do you think there is such a thing?'

Lisi thought of her mother's house and gave a slow smile. 'Oh, yes,' she said in a soft voice, and smiled. 'Very, very definitely.'

He smiled back, but the smile died on his lips as he forced himself to look away from the slender outline of her legs, relieved when Langley High Street came into view and he was able to draw up outside her office.

'Thanks very much,' she said as she began to push open the door. 'I enjoyed that!'

'No, thank *you*,' he said gravely, but as soon as she had slammed the door closed behind her, he made the car pull away. He didn't want to watch her confident young stride as she walked to the office, or the way her firm young breasts pushed against her soft, clinging sweater.

Lisi saw Philip seven, maybe eight times after that—on a purely professional basis. Sometimes Jonathon would accompany him on the viewings, but mostly it was her. For some reason she grew to know his tastes better than Jonathon. Often she would mentally reject a house once she had skimmed through the details, then phone him and suggest that he might like to see it.

'Do *you* like it?' he would demand.

She hesitated.

'*Do* you, Lisi?'

'I don't think it's quite what you're looking for.'

'Then I won't waste my time coming to see it.'

Leaving her wondering why she had been so foolish! Why hadn't she said that it was the most gorgeous place she had ever set eyes on?

Because then he wouldn't trust her judgement, and the fact that a man like Philip *did* meant more to her than it should have done.

She adored him, despite his emotional distance, but she kept it hidden from everyone—from Jonathon, from Saul Miller, even from her mother. And, especially, from Philip himself. Maybe she was aware that to fall for Philip Caprice would be batting right out of her league. And besides, it would be strictly unprofessional.

But she looked forward to his visits and they became the highlight of her life. Casually, she used to scour the diary to see when he was coming next, and—although she didn't make it look *too* obvious—she always felt her best on those days. Her hair always newly washed, and a subtle touching of fragrance behind her ears and at her wrists.

And then one glorious spring afternoon Philip walked into the office without his customary, flinty expression. He had loosened his tie and he seemed *lighter* in his mood, Lisi thought, though she wouldn't have dreamed of asking him why. That was not the way their relationship worked. They talked houses. Interest rates. Business trends.

'Hello, Philip.' She smiled.

He looked into her aquamarine eyes and smiled back. Carla had moved her fingers last night. The doctors were cautious, but quietly optimistic, and for the first time since the accident Philip had slept the night without waking. This morning he had awoken without the habitual tight knot of tension in his stomach. 'Hello, Lisi.' He smiled back. 'So what have you got for me?'

'I think you'll like it,' she said demurely.

The house she had rung him about was about as perfect as it was possible for a house to be. She had never heard Philip sound quite so enthusiastic, and the offer he made was accepted immediately. A rather more generous offer than usual, she noted, and briefly wondered what had made his mood quite so expansive.

It was getting on for six o'clock by the time he drove her back into Langley, and all the way along the lanes the hedges and trees were laced with the tender green buds of spring. He sighed. Spring. The time of new beginnings. He prayed that the signs were not misleading, and that there would be a new beginning for Carla.

Lisi heard the sigh, saw where he was looking. 'It's beautiful around this time of year, isn't it?'

He glanced across at her as she put her notebook back into her bag and snapped it shut.

He liked her. She worked hard and she didn't ask any questions. With Lisi he could relax, and he tried to think back to the last time he had done that. Really relaxed. 'I feel like celebrating,' he said.

'Well, then—why don't we? A quick drink won't hurt.' Her heart missed a beat while she waited to hear what he would say.

'Okay.' He changed down a gear. 'Where shall we go?'

'There's the pub or the hotel—either are good.'

'Yeah,' he said thoughtfully. 'I'm driving on to Somerset tomorrow, so I'm staying at the hotel.' Maybe they'd better go to the pub.

'I'll just have to ring my mother and tell her I'm going to be a little late.'

He raised his eyebrows, surprised. 'You live with your mother?'

Lisi smiled at his expression. How little of her he knew! 'Yes, I do.'

'Unusual, at your age.'

'I suppose so—but we get on very well.' No need to tell him that on her salary there was no way she could afford a place of her own, even if she had wanted to.

They went to the pub and settled down with their wine, but away from the usual professional boundaries which defined their relationship, Lisi found herself gulping hers down more quickly than usual.

He saw her empty glass and one elegant eyebrow was elevated. 'Another?'

'Please.' She nodded automatically, her eyes drinking in his tall, lean frame as he went up to buy her another drink.

She told him little anecdotes about village life, and when he smiled that slow, sexy smile she felt as though she had won first prize in a competition.

'You must let me buy *you* a drink now!' she offered, wishing that the evening could just go on and on.

He shook his dark, ruffled head. 'I'm fine. Really.'

'No, honestly—I insist! Just the one.' She smiled up at him. 'Equal rights for women, and all that!'

He laughed, thinking, Why not? 'Okay, Lisi,' he said gently. 'Just the one.'

In the cosy warmth of the bar, Lisi chatted away, and Philip was thinking that maybe it was getting just a little *too* cosy. He glanced at his watch. 'I guess it's about time we made a move,' he said, when he noticed that her cheeks had gone very pink and that she kept blinking her beautiful aquamarine eyes. 'Are you okay?' he frowned.

She nodded, even though the room was beginning to blur a little. 'I'm fine,' she gulped. But with a quick a glance at her watch she realised she'd drunk in record quick time. 'I'm just a bit whoozy. I guess I'm not used to drinking.'

'Have you eaten?' he demanded.

'No.'

His mouth tightened. A great influence he was turning out to be. And now she had acquired a deathly kind of pallor. He couldn't possibly send her home to her mother if she was half-cut, could he?

'Come on,' he said decisively, standing up and holding out his hand to her. 'You need something to soak up that alcohol.'

She clutched onto his hand gratefully and allowed him to lead her out of the pub. Outside the fresh air hit her like a sledgehammer, and she swayed against him and giggled.

Philip shot her a swift, assessing look. She needed food and then he needed *out*. What he did not need was some beautiful young woman brushing the delectable curves of her body so close to his.

But by the time they reached his hotel, Lisi had gone very pale indeed and Philip realised that he was trapped. He couldn't send her home like this, but neither could he see her managing to sit through a meal in a stuffy restaurant.

'You need to lie down,' he said grimly.

It sounded like heaven. 'Oh, yes, please,' she murmured indistinctly.

'Wait here while I get my keys,' he told her shortly, relieved to see that the foyer was completely empty, apart from the receptionist. And receptionists were trained to turn a blind eye, weren't they?

Lisi followed him up the stairs and walked with exaggerated care. She wasn't drunk, she told herself. Just feeling no pain!

Grimly, he pushed open the door, wondering just how he had managed to get himself into a situation which could look to the outside world as though he were intent on *seduction*. While nothing could be further than the truth. But he averted his eyes as she flopped down onto the bed like a puppet which had just had its strings cut.

'Kick your shoes off,' he growled.

The alcohol had loosened her inhibitions, and she giggled again as she obeyed his terse command, sneaking a look at him from between her slitted eyes and thinking how utterly gorgeous he looked. She wriggled and stretched her arms above her head with a blissful sigh.

The sight of her lying with such abandon on the scarlet silk coverlet was too much to bear. 'Go to sleep now,' he told her tightly. 'I'll wake you in a couple of hours and give you some food, then send you home.'

He made her sound like an abandoned puppy! thought Lisi. But her indignation faded into the distance as delicious sleep claimed her.

Philip sat moodily at the bar, sipping at a coffee and wondering whether he should ring the hospital. Maybe later. After Lisi had gone. And he *wanted* her gone!

But his body was telling him other things. Tormenting him with tantalising reminders of making love to a woman. He shifted uncomfortably on the bar stool, and would have taken the longest and coldest shower in the world had it not been for the fact that his room was occupied by the cause of his torment.

He waited a couple of hours and then ordered a plate of steak and chips to take upstairs to her. 'And a pot of strong coffee,' he added grimly. But it was with a heavy heart and an aching body as he slowly carried them into his room, and his breath froze in the back of his throat.

Because she was naked.

Naked in his bed.

Her arms were flung above her head, and part of the scarlet silk coverlet had slipped down to reveal one pert and perfect breast—pale and luscious and centred by a tiny thrusting peak of rose. Her long legs were accentuated by the coverlet which moulded itself against them and her clothes were in an untidy heap on the floor beside the bed, with a wispy thong lying uppermost.

Sweet heaven! Philip very nearly dropped the tray.

His heart was pounding fit to deafen him and he could feel the immediate jerk of a powerful erection as he shakily put the tray down on a small table.

He strode over to the bed, trying to use his anger to dampen down the overpowering need to join with her in the most fundamental way possible.

He reached his hand down to shake her by the shoulder but something happened along the way. His fingers irresistibly reached for her breast and he was appalled to find them stroking little circles, but unable to stop himself from finding the bud of her nipple and feeling it harden beneath his touch.

'Oh!' she breathed.

Eyes closed, still in the mists of sleep, Lisi writhed with pleasure beneath the bedclothes and the unconsciously sexy action nearly made him lose his mind. The blood roared in his head, his composure utterly shattered by the sight of a naked woman, warm and responsive and waiting in his bed.

With an unbearable effort, he tore his hand away from her nipple and moved it up to the soft silk of her shoulder, intending to shake her. But instead of shaking her, again he found his fingers kneading rhythmically against her cool flesh, urged on by the clamouring demands of his body.

'Wake up,' he ordered, in a low, furious voice. 'Wake up, Lisi!'

Lisi's eyes snapped open and she stared with disbelief into the dark, angry eyes of Philip. It took a second or two to get her bearings.

A strange bed.

A hotel room.

One drink too many.

'Oh, hell!' She sat bolt upright in bed and heard him utter something agonised beneath his breath, and she realised that she was wearing nothing at all and that Philip was staring at her bare breasts with a wild kind of furious hunger in his eyes.

'Put something on!' he snapped.

She was still befuddled by sleep. 'Where are my clothes?'

'How should I know where your bloody clothes are?' he roared. 'It wasn't me who took them off!'

Lisi blushed as vague memories came back to her. Feeling too hot and tossing her clothes to the ground with abandon. She had! Acutely aware of her nakedness and of the sound of Philip's quickened breath, she leaned over the side of the bed to hunt for them, and the movement made her breasts jiggle unfettered.

Suddenly Philip lost it completely. He moved towards her, tumbling onto the bed next to her and pulling her roughly into his arms to kiss her before he had the time or the inclination to think about the wisdom of his actions.

And once he had kissed her that was the beginning of the end—his starved senses and hungry body made sure of that.

The thong fell uselessly from her hand and there was a split second of doubt in Lisi's mind but that doubt fled the moment that he kissed her.

His mouth plundered hers as if it were the richest treasure

he had ever encountered and her lips parted for him immediately, moist and sweet and tasting faintly of wine.

Lisi's heart was beating so hard she thought that it might burst. This was every wish she'd ever had, every sweet dream come true. Philip. Here. In her arms. Her hands went up to his shoulders and felt the silk of his shirt beneath her fingertips. She was wearing nothing and he was covered up with all these clothes—it wasn't fair!

He lifted his head from hers and she could see that his eyes looked almost ebony in the lamplit room. 'Do you want to undress me, Lisi?' he asked unsteadily, because he couldn't trust himself to do it with any degree of finesse. Not when her breasts were peaking towards him like that and he longed to take one into his mouth and suckle her.

'Yes,' she murmured throatily, made bold by that look of raw need on his gorgeous face. Deftly, she began to unbutton his shirt, springing open the tiny buttons to reveal a golden-skinned torso sprinkled with a smattering of dark hair. She indolently ran the flat of her hand over the soft whorls, feeling him shudder beneath her as she did so, loving the power of having this big, handsome man respond so passionately to her.

He kissed her again. And again. Until she was mindless with longing—willingly pinned to the bed by his muscular frame and praying for him to make love to her properly.

Logic and reason had vanished from his mind—obliterated by the wet lick of her tongue as it flicked against his. If he didn't have her soon, he would explode. 'Undress me,' he commanded huskily. 'Undress me *now*, Lisi!'

She slid the shirt over his shoulders, anointing the flesh which she laid bare with soft little kisses which made him moan with pleasure beneath her mouth.

His belt came off easily, but her fingers faltered slightly when she was unzipping his trousers as she felt the formidable hardness of him brush against her palm.

'Don't touch me,' he pleaded. 'Not there. Not yet.'

He couldn't wait to be free of his clothes and yet he could hardly bear to watch the erotic vision she made as she pushed the covers off and sank down on her knees astride him, easing the trousers down slowly over the long, powerful shaft of his thighs. She eased them over his knees and further still, her hands brushing against the soft swell of his ankles and lingering there.

'Hurry up,' he pleaded.

Lisi skimmed one of his socks off—immensely flattered by his eagerness and yet slightly taken aback by it. Instinctively, she had known that he would be a passionate man, but she had expected him to exercise restraint as well. And steely control. Those were the qualities which seemed to fit more with the Philip Caprice she knew.

But it seemed that she had been completely wrong. She freed his foot from the second sock.

And then at last he was naked, too.

And aroused.

Very, very aroused.

Lisi swallowed. Surely he couldn't possibly... Surely she couldn't possibly... But then she bucked beneath his fingers as he slithered his middle finger along where she was so hot and slick and hungry. 'Oh!' she moaned in ecstasy.

He smiled, but it was a smile laced with a daunting kind of promise and Lisi felt the briefest shiver of apprehension as she saw the new and urgent tension which had entered his body.

'I want you,' he whispered.

'And I want you, too.'

'Now?' he teased. 'Or shall I play with you a little first?'

His provocative words made her melt even more. She had never been turned on so quickly, nor so thoroughly. There was no need for prolonged foreplay; she was ready.

And very, very willing. She put her arms around his neck and looked up at him with open invitation in her eyes.

'Let's play together,' she whispered back.

He groaned as he moved over her. It was like a dream—the most erotic dream he had ever encountered. He moved on top of her and could feel her shudder as he pressed right up against her burning heat. He delayed it for as long as he could—probably about a second—before powerfully thrusting into her and a deep, helpless cry was torn from his throat.

Lisi gasped aloud as she felt him fill her, but she wanted him deeper still, as deep as it was possible to go. She moved without thinking, lifting her legs right up so that her ankles were locked tightly around his neck, and he raised his head in a kind of dazed wonderment as he looked down at her.

'God, Lisi,' he groaned, and then thrust into her so deeply that she gasped again.

Through the stealthy lure of approaching orgasm, Philip heard warning bells ringing in his head, and he realised what he had never before failed to remember.

'Oh, God,' he groaned. 'Protection! Lisi, I never thought—' With a monumental effort he began to pull out, but Lisi only clenched her muscles, and gripped him even tighter and he shuddered. 'D-don't,' he commanded unsteadily.

'It's o-okay,' she gasped, because she had thought that she would die if he stopped what he was doing. 'It's safe.'

'You sure?'

She nodded. Of course she was sure. 'Make me come,' she begged, astonished by her lack of inhibition, but then something about Philip was making her feel this free. Freer than she had ever been in a man's arms.

'With pleasure,' he ground out, and moved inside her. He held back his own needs while he thrust into her over and over again, his mouth suckling at her breast, while his finger flicked tantalisingly over the tight, hot little core of her. And he whispered things to her, words so erotic, they were almost shocking.

Lisi was nearly crying with the pleasure—almost over-loaded with it—and then the crying became a shudder and she was calling out his name and telling him that he was the most perfect lover in the world as waves upon waves took her soaring.

He let himself go, sweat sheening his chest as it slicked against her breasts, and when it happened it was stronger and more intense than any other orgasm he had ever ex-perienced, so that even in the midst of pleasure, he felt the first shimmerings of guilt.

She felt him shuddering inside her for so long that she thought he would never stop. She wished that he wouldn't. Just go on filling her with his seed all night long. And only when he was completely spent did she let her legs drift down to lie on either side of him. With a satiated little smile, she lifted her head to kiss him but he turned away, as if her mouth contained poison, then rolled away from her completely, so that he was right on the other side of the bed.

Lisi's heart pounded.

Perhaps he was just tired. He always seemed to *look* tired. She would let him sleep and then he would reach for her again in the night, and…

She heard the sound of movement and saw that he was getting off the bed and reaching for his clothes.

Her heart pounded again. He couldn't be *leaving*! He couldn't! She swallowed down what was surely an irra-tional fear. He was obviously going to the bathroom—but he didn't need to put his clothes on to do that, surely? 'Philip?'

He finished buttoning up his shirt before he turned

around and when he did his face was as cold and as ex-
pressionless as flint. He raised his eyebrows. 'What?'

'You're not going?'

He was sickened with disgust at his lack of control, and
his mouth tightened. 'Yes.'

She stared at him without understanding. 'But why?' she
asked, in a mystified voice. 'Why are you leaving now?'

It hurt to say it, probably more than it hurt her to hear
it. 'Because I'm married,' he said, in a hard, cold voice.

He grabbed his jacket and his unopened overnight bag
and walked out without a backward glance.

And Lisi didn't see him again.

CHAPTER FOUR

PHILIP spent a sleepless night, tossing and turning, his thoughts full of Lisi and the effect of seeing her again.

He hadn't thought beyond his trip to Langley. He had just found himself on the road here, driven on by a burning need to tie up the loose ends of a regrettable liaison—so that he could put it behind him, once and for all.

But he had not reckoned on how he would feel if he saw her again. Part of him had thought that she might have moved on. Or settled down. Married some upstanding local and be well on the way to producing a brood of children. To his astonishment, she was still single.

And just the sight of her had been like a touch-paper to his senses. He still wanted her—wanted her more than he felt comfortable with, and, to judge from her response to his kiss, she wasn't exactly immune to him, either.

He owed her the truth, he realised. There would be no sense of closure for either of them until he had done that. *She* might have instigated what had happened, but he had gone into it more than willingly. She needed to know why he had feasted on her body and then just left her lying there without a second glance.

He glanced at his watch, but it was still early. He showered and dressed and drank some coffee before switching on his computer to check his e-mails. But he stared blankly at the untouched messages in his inbox and turned his head instead to study the forbidding grey of the winter sky.

Just as soon as the office opened he would go and see her. And tell her.

Marian Reece glanced up as the bell on the office door

rang and in walked the tall, expensively dressed man who had been talking so intently with Lisi the day before.

She smiled. 'Good morning! Mr Caprice, isn't it?'

Philip nodded and forced an answering smile. 'That's right. Philip Caprice.' He glanced around the office. 'Is Lisi around?'

Marian shook her head. 'Oh, no! She's finished now. For the Christmas holidays. She—' She seemed to change her mind about her next words. Instead, she said, 'But I'm sure that I can help you.'

He looked at her blankly. 'Help me?'

Marian studied him in bemusement. 'Well, you *did* say that you were interested in buying a house in this area!'

He narrowed his eyes. Did he? Wasn't the truth rather more complex than that? He had been doing business in the area, and something—the dreams, perhaps?—had prompted him to call in and see if Lisi Vaughan was still around. And she was—though wasn't there a part of him which wished she weren't? That had hoped she would have been long gone and then he could consign her to bitter-sweet memory? But at least the suggestion of house-hunting would legitimise his being here. 'That's right,' he said evenly. 'If you could let me have a few details to glance through.'

'Of course.' She gave a coy smile. 'I'll need to know your price range, though.'

He mentioned a sum that made her pupils dilate and she immediately reached for a sheaf of papers which stood neatly stacked on a corner of her desk. 'I *thought* you'd be looking at the top end of the market,' she said triumphantly, and handed them to him.

Philip glanced down at them without interest.

'The most attractive property we have on our books is The Old Rectory,' said Marian, straightening up and looking at him expectantly, but his gaze remained noncommittal. 'It's a beautiful old house, with a wealth of architectural detail—although it does require considerable updating, of course—'

'Why hasn't it sold already?' he cut in.

Marian blinked. 'Sorry?'

'If it's so beautiful, then why hasn't it been snatched up?'

Marian gave a little cough and lowered her voice. 'Because it's unrealistically priced,' she admitted.

'Then get the vendors to lower it.'

'They're reluctant.' She sighed, and pulled a face. 'It's a divorce sale, you see, and they need every penny they can get. I've told them that they may not get a buyer unless they're prepared to be realistic, but you know what people are.'

He nodded and gave an impatient smile, eager to be away. 'Listen, I need to see Lisi. Can you tell me where she lives?'

Marian hesitated. 'I'm…I'm not sure that I should. She might not want me to.'

Philip met her eyes with an unwavering stare. 'Oh, I think she would,' he said pleasantly. 'But, of course, if you won't tell me—then I'll just have to find out for myself. Only it would save me a little time.' He gave her a lazy smile. 'Giving me more opportunity to look at houses.'

There was a long pause while she considered the subtext behind his words, and then she nodded. 'She lives at Cherry Tree Cottage—it's on Millbank Lane. A bright blue front door—it's easy enough to find.'

He folded up the house details and slid them into the pocket of his overcoat. 'Thanks very much.'

Marian looked at him anxiously. 'I don't know whether I should have told you.'

He gave a tight smile. 'I would have found her anyway.'

*   *   *

Lisi had just finished pinning the flouncy paper frill onto the birthday cake when there was a knock at the door, and she sighed. What she *didn't* need at the moment was an interruption! There were a million and one things to do before Tim's party—when the house would be invaded by five of his friends and she would have her work cut out to prevent six small boys from wrecking her little home!

She brushed some stray icing sugar from her hands and went to the front door, and there, standing on the step, was Philip, and her heart lurched with a combination of apprehension and lust.

He looked pretty close to irresistible, dressed casually in jeans which emphasised the long, muscular thrust of his thighs and a soft grey sweater which made the green eyes look even more dazzling than usual. He wore an old-fashioned flying jacket, and the sheepskin and worn leather only added to his rugged appeal.

She thought of Tim in the sitting room, watching a video, and the lurch of her heart turned into a patter of alarm.

'Hello, Philip,' she said calmly. 'This is a surprise.'

He gazed at her steadily. 'Is it? Surely you didn't think that I was going to go away without speaking to you again, Lisi?'

'I have nothing to say to you.'

'But I do,' he said implacably.

He can't make you do anything, she told herself. 'I'm afraid that it isn't convenient right now.'

He let his eyes rove slowly over her, and the answering flood of heat made him wish that he hadn't.

Her dark hair was scraped back from her face into a pony-tail and she wore cheap clothes—nothing special—a pair of baggy cotton trousers and an old sweater which clung to the soft swell of her breasts. There was a fine line of flour running down her cheek which made him think of warpaint.

And she looked like dynamite.

'Been cooking, have you?'

'*Am* cooking,' she corrected tartly. 'Busy cooking.'

'Mum-mee!'

Lisi froze as green eyes lanced through her in a disbelieving question.

'Mum-mee!' A child who was Lisi's very image appeared, and Tim came running out from the sitting room and up to the door, turning large, interested blue eyes up at the stranger on the doorstep. 'Hello!'

Lisi had always been proud of her son's bright and outgoing nature—she had brought him up to be confident—but at that moment she despaired of it. Why couldn't he have been shy and retiring, like most other boys his age? 'I really must go, Philip, you can see I'm really—'

He ignored her completely. 'Hello,' Philip said softly as he looked down at the shiny black head. 'And what's your name?'

The boy smiled. 'I'm Tim, and it's my birthday!' he said. 'Who are you?'

'I'm Philip. A friend of Mummy's.'

Tim screwed his eyes up. 'Mummy's boyfriend?'

Lisi saw the cold look of distaste which flickered across his face, and flinched.

'Does Mummy have lots of boyfriends, then?' Philip asked casually.

'*Tim*,' said Lisi, a note of desperation making her voice sound as though it was about to crack, 'why don't you go and colour in that picture that Mummy drew for you earlier?'

'But, *Mum*-mee—'

'Please, darling,' she said firmly. 'And you can have a biscuit out of the tin—only one, mind—and Mummy will come and help you in a minute, and we can organise all the games for your party. Won't that be fun? Run along now, darling.'

Thank heavens the suggestion of an unsolicited biscuit had captured his imagination! He gave Philip one last, curious look and then scampered back towards the sitting room.

Lisi tried to meet the condemnatory green stare without flinching. 'It's his birthday,' she explained. 'And I'm busy organising—'

'So *that* was why you had to ring your mother,' he observed softly.

It was not the aggressive question she had been expecting and dreading. She stared at him uncomprehendingly. *'What?'*

'The night you slept with me,' he said slowly. 'I wondered why you should bother to do that, when we were only *supposedly* going for a quick drink,' he added witheringly. 'I guess you had to arrange for your mother to babysit. Poor little soul,' he finished. 'When Mummy jumps into bed with a man whenever the opportunity presents itself.'

For a moment, Lisi couldn't work out what he was talking about, and then his words began to make sense. Tim was a tall boy, as Marian had said. He looked older than his years. And Philip didn't even suspect that the child might be his. God forgive me, she thought. But this is something I have to do. For all our sakes. He hates me. He thinks the worst of me—he's made that heartbreakingly clear. What good would it do *any* of us if he found out the truth?

'I have never neglected my son, Philip,' she said truthfully.

Did this make them quits? All the time he hadn't told her about Carla, lying desperately sick in her hospital bed— Lisi had carried an awesome secret, too. A baby at home. And who else? he wondered. 'So where's the father?' he demanded. 'Was he still on the scene when you stripped off and climbed into my bed?'

'How dare you say something like that?'

'It was a simple question.'

She jerked her head in the direction of the sitting room door. 'Just keep your voice down!' she hissed, and then met the fury in his eyes. 'Oh, what's the point of all this? You've made your feelings about me patently clear, Philip. There is nothing between us. There never was—other than a night of mad impetuosity. We both know that. End of story. And now, if you don't mind—I really do have a party to organise.'

He made to turn away. Hadn't a part of him nurtured a tiny, unrealistic hope that her behaviour that night had been a one-off—that it had been something about *him* which had made her so wild and so free in his bed? And all the time she'd had a child by another man! It was a fact of modern life and he didn't know why he should feel so bitterly disappointed. But he did.

'Goodbye, Philip.' Her overwhelming feeling was one of relief, but there was regret as well. She couldn't have him— she would never have him—not when his fundamental lack of respect for her ran so deep. But that didn't stop a tiny, foolish part of her from aching for what could never be.

He looked deep into her eyes and some sixth sense told him that all was not how it seemed. Something was not right. She was tense. Nervous. More nervous than she had any right to be, and he wondered why.

She started to close the door when he said, 'Wait!'

There was something so imperious in his command, something so darkly imperative in the glacial green gaze that Lisi stopped in her tracks. 'What?'

'You didn't say how old Tim was.'

She felt the blood freeze in her veins, but she kept her face calm. 'That's because you didn't ask.'

'I'm asking now.'

A thousand thoughts began to make a scrabbled journey through her mind. Could she carry it off? Would he see through the lie if she told him that Tim was four? It was credible—everybody said that he could easily pass for a four-year-old.

Her hesitation told him everything, as did the blanching of colour from her already pale face. He felt the slow, steady burn of disbelief. And anger. 'He's mine, isn't he?'

If she had thought that seeing him again was both nightmare and dream, then this was the nightmare sprung into worst possible life. She stared at him. 'Philip—'

'*Isn't* he?' he demanded, in a low, harsh voice which cut through her like a knife.

She leant on the door for support, and nodded mutely.

'Say it, Lisi! Go on, say it!'

'Tim is your son,' she admitted tonelessly, and then almost recoiled from the look of naked fury in his eyes.

'You bitch,' he said softly. 'You utter little bitch.'

She had played this unlikely scenario in her mind many times. Philip would magically appear and she would tell him about Tim, but she had never imagined a reaction like this—with him staring at her with a contempt so intense that she could have closed her eyes and wept.

'Go away,' she whispered. 'Please, just go away.'

'I'm not going anywhere. I want to know everything.'

'Philip.' She sucked in a ragged breath. Should she appeal to his better nature? Surely he must have one? 'I *will* talk to you, of course I will—'

'Well, thanks for nothing!' he scorned.

'But not now. I can't. Tim will come out again in a minute if I'm not back and it isn't fair—'

'*Fair?*' he echoed sardonically. 'You think that what you have done is *fair*? To deny me all knowledge of my own flesh and blood? And then to lie about it?'

'I did not lie!' she protested.

'Oh, yes, you did,' he contradicted roughly. 'It was—to use your own words, my dear Lisi—a lie by omission, wasn't it? Just now, when I asked you his age, you thought about concealing it from me.' His mouth hardened into a cruel, contemptuous line. 'But I'm afraid your hesitation gave you away.'

'Just go,' she begged. 'Don't let Tim hear this. Please.'

He hardened his heart against the appeal in her eyes. He had lived with death and loss and all the time she had brought new life into the world and had jealously kept that life to herself. As if they had stumbled across unexpected treasure together, and she had decided to claim it all for herself.

'What time does his party finish?'

She could scarcely think. 'At around s-six.'

'And what time does he go to bed?'

'He'll be tired tonight. I should be able to settle him down by seven.'

'I'll come at seven.'

She shook her head. 'Can't we leave it until tomorrow?' she pleaded.

He gave her a look of pure scorn. 'It has already been left three years too long!'

'Then one more night won't make any difference. Sleep on it, Philip—you won't feel so…so…angry about it in the morning.'

But he couldn't ever imagine being rid of the rage which was smouldering away at the pit of his stomach. 'How very naive you are, Lisi—if you think that I'll agree to that. Either I come round tonight once Tim has gone to sleep, or I march straight in there now and tell him exactly what his relationship to me is.'

'You wouldn't do that.'

'Just try me,' he said, in a voice of soft menace.

Lisi swallowed. 'Okay. I'll see you here. Tonight. Unless…' she renewed the appeal in her eyes '—unless you'd rather meet on…neutral territory? I could probably get a babysitter.'

But he shook his head resolutely. 'Thanks, but no thanks,' he said coldly. 'Maybe I might like to look in on my sleeping son, Lisi. Surely you wouldn't deny me that?'

My sleeping son. The possessive way that he said it made Lisi realise that Philip Caprice was not intending to be an absentee father. Already! How the hell was she going to cope with all the implications of *that*?

But what about Tim? prompted the voice of her conscience. What about him?

'No, I won't deny you that,' she told him quietly. 'I'll see you here tonight, around seven.'

He gave a brief, mock-courteous nod and then turned on his heel, walking away from her without a second glance, the way he had done the night his son had been conceived.

She shut the door before he was halfway down the path, and looked down to see that her hands were shaking.

She waited until her breath had stopped coming in short, anxious little breaths, but as she caught a glance at her reflection in the mirror she saw that her face was completely white, her eyes dark and frightened, like a trapped animal.

I must pull myself together, she thought. She had a son and a responsibility to him. Today was his party—his big day. She had already messed up in more ways than one. She mustn't let the complex world of adult relationships ruin it for him.

She forced a smile onto her lips and hoped that it didn't look too much like a grimace, and then she opened the door to the sitting room, where her beloved son sat with his dark head bent over his colouring, his little tongue from between his teeth, just the way hers did. He's my son, too, she told herself fiercely. Not just Philip's.

'Hello, darling,' she said softly. 'Shall Mummy come and help for a bit?'

Tim looked up, his eyes narrowed in that clever way of his, and Lisi stared at him with a sudden, dawning recognition. His eyes might be blue like hers, but that expression was pure Philip. Why had she never seen it before? Because she had deliberately blinded herself to it as too painful?

'Mum-mee,' said Tim, and put his crayon down firmly on top of the paper. 'Who was that man?'

Not now, she told herself. How he must be told was going to take some working out.

'Oh, he's just a friend, darling,' she said, injecting her voice with a determined cheerfulness. 'A friend of Mummy's.'

But the words rang hollow in her ears.

CHAPTER FIVE

THE hours ticked by so slowly while Philip waited. He felt as though the whole landscape of his life had been altered irrevocably—as if someone had detonated a bomb and left a familiar place completely unrecognisable.

He went through the motions of working. He faxed the States. He replied to his e-mails. He made phone-calls to his London office, and it seemed from the responses given by his staff that he must have sounded quite normal.

But he didn't feel in the least normal. He had just discovered that he was the biological father of a child who was a complete unknown to him and he knew that he was going to have to negotiate some paternal rights.

Whether Lisi Vaughan liked it or not.

He deliberately turned his thoughts away from her. He wasn't going to think about her. Thinking about her just made his rage grow, and rage would not help either of them come to some kind of amicable agreement about access.

Amicable?

The word mocked him. How could the two of them ever come to some kind of friendly understanding after what had happened?

He went for a long walk as dusk began to fall, looking up into the heavy grey clouds and wondering if the threatened snow would ever arrive, and at seven prompt he was knocking on her door.

She didn't answer immediately and his mouth tightened. If the secretive little witch thought that she could just hide inside and he would just go away again, then she was in for an unpleasant surprise.

The door opened, and he was unprepared for the impact of seeing her all dressed up for a party. Red dress. Red shoes. Long, slim legs encased in pale stockings which had a slight sheen to them. He had never seen her in red before, but scarlet had been the backdrop to her beauty when she had lain with such abandon on his bed. Scarlet woman, he thought, and felt the blood thicken in his veins.

'You'd better come in,' said Lisi.

'With pleasure,' he answered, grimly sarcastic.

She opened the door wider to let him in, but took care to press herself back against the wall, as far away from him as possible. She was only hanging onto her self-possession by a thread, and if he came anywhere near her she would lose it completely. But he still came close enough for her to catch the faint drift of his aftershave—some sensual musky concoction which clamoured at her senses.

He followed her into the sitting room, where the debris from the party still littered the room. He wondered how many children there had been at the party. Judging by the clutter left behind it could easily have run into tens.

There were balloons everywhere, and scrunched up wrapping paper piled up in the bin. Half-eaten pieces of cake and untouched sandwiches lay scattered across the paper cloth which covered the table.

Philip frowned. 'Weren't they hungry?'

'They only ever eat the crisps.'

'I see.' He looked around the room in slight bemusement. 'They certainly know how to make a mess, don't they?'

Lisi gave a rueful smile, thinking that maybe they *could* be civil to one another. 'I should have cleared it away, but I wanted to read Tim a story from one of his new books.'

The mention of Tim's name reminded him of why he was there. 'Very commendable,' he observed sardonically.

'Can I…?' She forced herself to say it, even though his manner was now nothing short of hostile. But she had told herself over and over again that nothing good would come out of making an enemy of him, even though the look on his face told her that she was probably most of the way there. 'Can I get you a drink?'

'In a minute. Firstly, I want to see Tim.'

She steeled herself not to react to that autocratic demand. 'He's only just gone to sleep,' she said. 'What if he wakes?'

'I'll be very quiet. And anyway, what if he *does* wake?'

'Don't you know *anything* about children?' she asked, but one look at his expression made her wonder how she could have come out with something as naive and as hurtful as that.

'Actually, no.' He bit the words out precisely. 'Because up until this morning, I didn't realise that I might have to.'

'Just wait until he's in a really deep sleep,' she said, desperately changing the subject. 'He might be alarmed if he wakes up to find a strange man…' Her words tailed off embarrassedly.

He gave a bitter laugh. 'A strange man in his room?' he completed acidly. 'You mean it doesn't happen nightly, Lisi?'

It was one insult too many and on top of all the tensions of the day it was just too much. Her hand flew up to his face and she slapped him, hard. There was a dull ringing sound as her palm connected, but he didn't react at all, just stood there looking at her, his expression unreadable.

'Feel better now?'

She bit her lip in horror. She had never raised her hand to anyone in her life! 'What do you think?'

He turned away. He didn't want her looking at him all vulnerable and lost like that. He wanted to steel his heart against her pale beauty and the black hair which streamed down her back, tied back with a scarlet ribbon which matched the dress. 'You don't want to hear what I think,' he said heavily. 'I'll take that drink now.'

She went into the kitchen and took wine from the fridge and handed him the bottle, along with two glasses. 'Maybe you could just open that, and I'll clear up a little,' she said.

He sat down in one of the squashy old armchairs and began to open the wine, but his eyes followed her as she moved around the room, deftly clearing the table and bundling up all the leftover party food into the paper cloth.

He wished that she would go and put on the baggy trousers she had been wearing this morning. The sight of the shiny red material stretching over the pert swell of her bottom was making him have thoughts he would rather not have. He was here to talk about his son, not fantasise about taking her damned dress off.

She had lit the fire, and the room flickered with the shadowed reflections of the flames. On the now-cleared table he saw her place a big copper vase containing holly, whose bright berries matched the scarlet of her dress. It was, he thought, with bitter irony, a delightfully cosy little scene.

She took the glass of wine he handed her and sat in the chair facing his, her knees locked tightly together, wishing that she had had the opportunity to change from a dress which was making her uncomfortably aware of the tingling sensation in her breasts. Just what did he do to her simply by looking? She twisted the stem of her glass round and round. 'What shall we drink to?'

He studied her for a long moment. 'How about to truth?'

She took a mouthful and the warmth of the liquor started to unravel the knot of tension which had been coiled up in the pit of her stomach all day. She stared at him. 'Do you really think that *you* have a monopoly on truth? Why the hell do you think I didn't contact you and tell you when I found out I was pregnant?'

'What goes on in your mind is a complete mystery to me.'

Because you don't know me, thought Lisi sadly. And now you never will. Philip's opinion of her would always be distorted. He saw her as some kind of loose woman who would fall into bed with just about any man. Or as a selfish mother who would deliberately keep him from his own flesh and blood.

'Think about the last words you said to me,' she reminded him softly, but the memory still had the power to make her flinch. 'You told me you were married. What was I supposed to do? Turn up on your doorstep with a bulging stomach and announce that you were about to be a daddy? What if your wife had answered the door? I can't imagine that she would have been particularly overjoyed to hear that!'

He didn't respond for a moment. He had come here this morning intending to tell her about the circumstances which had led to that night. About Carla. But his discovery of Tim had driven that far into the background. There were only so many revelations they could take in one day. Wouldn't talking about his wife at this precise moment muddy the waters still further? Tim must come first.

'You could have telephoned me,' he pointed out. 'The office had my number. You could have called me any time.'

'The look on your face as you walked out that night made me think that you would be happy never to see me again. The disgust on your face told its own story.'

Self-disgust, he thought bitterly. Disgusted at his own weakness and disgusted by the intensity of the pleasure he had experienced in her arms. A relative stranger's arms.

He put the wineglass down on the table and his eyes glittered with accusation.

'The situation should never have arisen,' he ground out. 'You shouldn't have become pregnant in the first place.'

'Tell me something I don't know! I didn't exactly *choose* to get pregnant!'

'Oh, really?' The accusation in his voice didn't waver. 'You told me that it was safe.' He gave a hollow laugh. 'Safe? More fool me for believing you.'

Her fingers trembling so much that she was afraid that she might slop wine all over her dress, Lisi put her own glass down on the carpet. 'Are you saying that I lied, Philip?'

His cool, clever eyes bored into her.

'Facts are facts,' he said coldly. 'I realised that we were not using any protection. I offered to stop—' He felt his groin tensing as he remembered just when and how he had offered to stop, and a wave of desire so deep and so hot swept over him that it took his breath away. He played for time, slowly picking up his glass and lifting it to his lips until he had his feelings under control once more.

'I offered to stop,' he continued, still in that hard, cold voice. 'And you assured me that it was safe. Just how was it safe, Lisi? Were you praying that it would be—because you were so het-up you couldn't bear me to stop? Or were you relying on something as outrageously unreliable as the so-called ''safe'' period?'

'Do you really think I'd take risks like that?' she demanded.

'Who knows?'

She gave a short laugh. If she had entertained any lingering doubt that there might be some fragment of affection for her in the corner of his heart, then he had dispelled it completely with that arrogant question.

'For your information—I was on the pill at the time—'

'Just in case?' he queried hatefully.

'Actually—' But she stopped short of telling him why. She was under no obligation to explain that, although she had broken up with her steady boyfriend a year earlier, the pill had suited her and given her normal periods for the first time in her life and she had seen no reason to stop taking it. 'It's none of your business why I was taking it.'

I'll bet, he thought grimly. 'So why didn't it work?'

'Because...' She sighed. 'I guess because I had a bout of sickness earlier that week. In the heat of the moment, it slipped my mind. It was a million-to-one chance—'

'I think that the odds were rather higher than that, don't you?' He raised his eyebrows insolently. 'You surely must have known that there was a possibility that it would fail?'

Unable to take any more of the cold censure on his face, she leaned over to throw another log on the fire and it spat and hissed back at her like an angry cat. 'What do you want me to say? That I couldn't bear for you to stop?' Because that was the shameful truth. At the time she had felt as if the world would come to an abrupt and utter end if he'd stopped his delicious love-making. But she hadn't *consciously* taken a risk.

'And couldn't you, Lisi? Bear me to stop?'

She met his eyes. The truth he had wanted, so the truth he would get. 'No. I couldn't. Does that flatter your ego?'

His voice was cold. 'My ego does not need flattering. And anyway—' he topped up both their glasses '—how it happened is now irrelevant—we can't turn the clock back, can we?'

His words struck a painful chord and she knew that she had to ask him the most difficult question of all. Even if she didn't like the answer. 'And if you could?' she queried softly. '*Would* you turn the clock back?'

He stared at her in disbelief. Was she really that naive? 'Of course I would!' he said vehemently, though the way her mouth crumpled when he said it made him feel distinctly uncomfortable. 'Wouldn't you?'

She gave him a sad smile. He would never understand—not in a million years. 'Of course I wouldn't.'

'You *wouldn't*?'

'How could I?' she asked simply. 'When the encounter gave me a son.'

He noted her use of the word *encounter*. Which told him precisely how *she* regarded what had happened that night. Easy come. His mouth twisted. Easy go. She certainly had not bothered to spare his feelings, but then why should she? He had not spared hers. There was no need for loyalty between them—nothing at all between them, in fact, other than an inconvenient physical attraction.

And a son.

'He looks like you,' he observed.

'That's what everyone says,' said Lisi serenely, and saw to her amazement that a flicker of something very much like…disappointment…crossed his features. 'And it's a good thing he does, isn't it?' she asked him quietly.

'Meaning?'

'Well, I would hate him to resemble a father who wished that the whole thing never happened.'

'Lisi, you are wilfully misunderstanding me!' he snapped.

She shook her head. 'I don't think so. You would wish him unborn, if you could.'

'You can't wish someone unborn!' he remonstrated, and then his voice unexpectedly gentled. 'And if I really thought the whole situation so regrettable, then why am I here? Why didn't I just stay away when I found out, as you so clearly wanted me to?'

She shrugged. 'I don't know.'

'Then I'll tell you.' He leaned forward in the chair. 'Obviously the circumstances of his conception are not what I would have chosen—'

'What a delightful way to phrase it,' put in Lisi drily.

'But Tim is here now. He exists! He is half mine—'

'You can't cut him up in portions as you would a cake!' she protested.

'Half mine in terms of genetic make-up,' he continued inexorably.

'Now you're making him sound like Frankenstein,' observed Lisi, slightly hysterically.

'Don't be silly! I want to watch him grow,' said Philip, and his voice grew almost dreamy. 'To see him develop into a man. To influence him. To teach him. To be a father to him.'

Lisi swallowed. This didn't sound like the occasional contact visit to her. But she had denied him access for three whole years, wouldn't it sound unspeakably mean to object to that curiously possessive tone which had deepened his voice to sweetest honey?

And besides, what was she worrying about? He lived in London, for heaven's sake—and, although Langley was commutable from the capital, she imagined that he would soon get tired of travelling up and down the country to see Tim.

She knew how fickle men could be. She thought of Dave, her best friend Rachel's husband, who had deserted Rachel just over a year ago. They had a son of Tim's age and Dave's visits to see him had dwindled to almost nothing. And that was from a man who had fallen in love with and married the mother of his child. Who had seen that child grow from squalling infant to chubby toddler. If *he* had lost interest—then how long would she give Philip before he tired of fatherhood?

'I'd like to see him now, please.'

This time there was no reason not to agree to his request, but Lisi felt almost stricken by a reluctance to do so. Something was going to end right here and now, she realised. For so long it had been just her and Tim—a unit which went together as perfectly as peaches and cream. No one

else had been able to lay claim on him and, since her
mother had died, she had considered herself to be his only
living relation. He was hers. All hers—and now she was
going to have to relinquish part of him to his father.

A lump rose in the back of her throat and she swallowed
it down.

Philip was staring at her from between narrowed eyes.
Did her eyes glitter with the promise of tears? 'Are you
okay?'

'Of course I'm okay,' she answered unconvincingly.
'Why shouldn't I be?'

'Because you've gone so pale.'

'I *am* pale, Philip—you know that.' He had told her so
that night in his arms. 'Pale as the moon,' he had whispered, as his lips had burned fire along her flesh. 'Come
with me,' she said slowly.

The two of them walked with exaggerated care towards
the closed door with its hand-painted sign saying, 'Tim's
Room'.

Lisi pushed the door open quietly and tiptoed over to the
bed, where a little hump lay tucked beneath a Mickey-
Mouse duvet, and Philip was surprised by the clamour of
a far-distant memory. So she still had a thing about Disney,
did she?

He went to stand beside her, and looked down, unprepared for the kick of some primitive emotion deep inside
him. The sleeping child looked almost unbearably peaceful,
with only one small lock of dark hair obscuring the pure
lines of a flawless cheek. His lashes were long, he realised—as long as Lisi's—and his mouth was half open as
he took in slow, steady breaths.

'So innocent,' he said, very softly. 'So very innocent.'

It was such a loaded word, and Lisi felt a strange, useless
yearning. He thought *her* the very antithesis of innocence,
didn't he? If only it could be different. But she knew in

her heart that it never could. She nodded, gazing down with pride at the shiny-clean hair of her son. Their son. He looked scrubbed-clean and contented. Good enough to eat.

She stole a glance at Philip, who was studying Tim so intently that she might as well not have existed. Strange now how *his* profile should remind her of Tim's. Had that been because he had not been around to make any comparisons? How much else of Tim was Philip? she wondered. What untapped genetic secrets lay dormant in that sweet, sleeping form?

Philip turned his head and their eyes made contact in a moment of strange, unspoken empathy. She read real sadness in *his* eyes. And regret—and wondered what he saw in hers.

He probably didn't care.

She put her finger onto her lips and beckoned him back out. She did *not* want Tim to wake and to demand to know what this man was doing here. Again. She shut the door behind them and went back into the sitting room, where Philip stood with his back to the fire, looking to all intents and purposes as if he were the master of the house.

But he never would be. She must remember that. In fact, it was almost laughable to try to imagine Philip Caprice living in this little house with her and Tim. The ceiling seemed almost too low to accommodate him, he was so tall. She tried to picture them all cramming into the tiny bathroom in the mornings and winced.

'Would you like some more wine?' she asked.

He shook his head. 'No, thanks. Coffee would be good, though.'

She was glad of the opportunity to escape to the kitchen and busy herself with the cafetière. She carried it back in with a plate of biscuits to find him standing where she had left him, only now he was staring deep into the heart of the fire with unseeing eyes.

He took the cup from her and gave a small smile of appreciation. 'Real coffee,' he murmured.

At that moment she really, really hated him. Did he have any idea just how *patronising* that sounded? 'What did you expect?' she asked acidly. 'The cheapest brand of instant on the market?'

He shook his head, still dazed by the emotional impact of seeing his son. 'You're right—if anything was cheap it was my remark.'

And what about the others? she wanted to cry out. The intimation that she had deliberately got pregnant. Wasn't that the cheapest remark a man could ever make to a woman? He wasn't taking *those* back, was he?

'So who else knows?' he demanded.

Lisi blinked. 'Knows what?'

'About Tim,' he said impatiently. 'How many others are privy to the secret I was excluded from?

She shook her head. 'No one. No one knows.'

'No-one at all?' he queried disbelievingly.

'No. Why should they? As far as anyone knew—we simply had a professional relationship. Even Jonathon thought that—and nobody was aware that I went up to your room at the hotel that night.' She shuddered, thinking how sordid that sounded. She bit her lip. 'The only person I told was my mother, just before she died.'

'You told her the whole story?' he demanded incredulously.

Again, she shook her head. 'I edited it more than a bit.'

'Was she shocked?'

Lisi shrugged. 'A little, but I made it sound…' She hesitated. She had made it sound as though she had been in love with him, and that bit she had found surprisingly easy. 'I made it sound rather more than it had been.' And her mother had pleaded with her to contact him. But then the bit she had omitted to tell her mother had been that Philip had already been married.

He looked at her and gave a heavy smile. 'My parents will want to meet him,' he said, wondering just how he was going to tell his elderly parents that he, too, was a parent.

'Your p-parents?'

His eyes were steady. 'But of course. What did you expect?'

What *had* she expected? Well, for one thing—she had expected to live the rest of her life without ever seeing Philip again. 'I don't know,' she admitted. 'I haven't really thought it through.'

'He's in my life now, too, Lisi,' he said simply. 'And I don't come in a neat little box marked ''Philip Caprice''— to be opened up at will and shut again when it suits you. I have family who will want to get to know him. And friends, too.'

And girlfriends? she wondered. Maybe even one particular girlfriend who was very special to him? Maybe even… She raised troubled aquamarine eyes to his. 'Have you married, again, Philip?' she asked quietly.

'No.'

She felt the fierce, triumphant leap of her heart and despaired at herself. Fool, she thought. Fool! 'So where do we go from here?'

He despised himself for the part of him which wanted to say, Let's go to bed—because even though the distance between them was so vast that he doubted whether it could ever be mended, that didn't stop him from being turned on by her. He shifted uncomfortably in the chair. Very turned on indeed. He met her questioning gaze with a look of challenge. 'You tell Tim about me as soon as possible.'

Her mouth fell open. '*Tell* him?'

'Of course you tell him!' he exploded softly. 'I'm back, Lisi—and I'm staking my claim.'

It sounded so territorial. So loveless. 'Oh, I see,' she said slowly.

He narrowed his eyes. 'Just how were you planning to explain to him about his father? If I hadn't turned up.'

'I honestly don't know. It's not something I ever gave much thought to. He's so young, and whenever he asked I just said that Mummy and Daddy broke up before he was born and that I hadn't seen you since.' It had seemed easier to bury her head in the sand than to confront such a painful issue. 'Maybe one day I might have told him who his real father was.'

'When?' he demanded. 'When he was five? Six? Sixteen?'

'When the time was right.'

'And maybe the time never *would* have been right, hmm, Lisi? Did you think you could get away with keeping me anonymous for the rest of his life, so that the poor kid would never know he had a father?'

She met the burning accusation in his eyes and couldn't pretend. Not about this. 'I don't know,' she whispered.

He rose to his feet. 'Well, just make sure you do it. And soon. I don't care how you do it—just tell him!'

She nodded. She wanted him gone now—with as long a space until his next visit as possible. 'And when will we see you again? Some time after Christmas?'

He heard the hopeful tinge to her question and gave a short laugh. 'Hard luck, Lisi,' he said grimly. 'I'm afraid that I'm not going to just conveniently disappear from your life again. I'm intending to be around quite a bit. Just call it making up for lost time, if it makes you feel better. And it's Christmas very soon.'

'Christmas?' she echoed, in a horrified whisper.

'Sure.' His mouth hardened into an implacable line. 'I was tempted to buy him a birthday present today, but I didn't want to confuse him. However, there's only a week to go until Christmas and some time between now and then he needs to know who I am.' His eyes glittered. 'Because you can rest assured that I will be spending part of the holiday with him.'

She wanted to cry out and beg him not to disrupt the relatively calm order of her life, but as she looked into Philip's strong, cold face she knew that she would be wasting her breath. He wasn't going to go away, she recognised, and if she tried to stop him then he would simply bring in the best lawyers that money could buy in order to win contact with his child. She didn't need to be told to know that.

'Understood?' he asked softly.

'Do I have any choice?'

'I think you know the answer to that. Don't worry about seeing me to the door. I'll let myself out.'

As if in a dream she watched him go and shut the front door quietly behind him, and only when she had heard the last of his footsteps echoing down the path did she allow herself to sink back down onto the chair and to bury her head in her hands and take all that was left to her.

The comfort of tears.

CHAPTER SIX

LISI was woken by the sound of the telephone ringing, and as she picked it up she was aware that something was not as it should be.

'Hello?'

'Lisi, it's Marian.'

Sleepily, Lisi wondered what her boss was doing ringing her this early in the morning... She sat bolt upright in bed. That was it! That was what was not right! She had over-slept—she could tell that much by the light which was filtering through the curtains. 'What time is it?' she asked urgently.

'Nine-thirty, why—?'

'Wait there!' swallowed Lisi, and left the receiver on the bed while she rushed into Tim's bedroom. What was the matter with him? Why hadn't he woken at his usual un-earthly hour? Had Philip Caprice climbed in through one of the windows in the middle of the night and kidnapped his son?

But to her relief her son was sitting on his bed, engrossed in playing with some of his new birthday toys. He looked up as Lisi flew into the room, and smiled.

''Lo, Mum-mee,' he said happily. 'Me playing with trac-tor!'

'So I see! And a lovely tractor it is too, darling,' said Lisi, charging across the room to drop a kiss on top of his head. 'Mummy's just talking to Marian on the telephone and then we'll have a great big breakfast together!'

But Tim's head was bent over his toy again and he was busy making what he imagined to be tractor noises.

On the way back to speak to Marian, Lisi reflected how different things felt this morning. She no longer felt weak or intimidated by Philip. He had decided that he wanted contact and there was nothing she could do about it—but he could do all the legwork. She would just be polite. Icily polite.

Because during the middle of her largely sleepless night she had come to her senses and a great sense of indignation had made her softly curse his name.

He had been so busy attacking her that she hadn't really had time to consider that he had shown no remorse about betraying his wife. Nor any shame for his part in what had happened. Philip obviously wanted to make her the scapegoat—well, tough! He should look to himself first!

She picked the phone back up. 'Hello, Marian—are you still there?'

'Just about,' came the dry reply. 'Where did you go—Scotland?'

'Very funny.'

'You sound more cheerful today,' observed Marian.

'I am,' said Lisi. '*Much* happier!'

There was a short pause. 'I don't know if you're going to be after what I'm about to tell you.'

A sudden sense of foreboding filled Lisi with dread. This was something to do with Philip. 'What is it?'

'It's Philip Caprice.'

Exasperation and impatience made Lisi feel like screaming—until she reminded herself that the worst had already been exposed. There was nothing he could do to hurt and upset her now. 'What now?' she asked.

'He wants you to show him round a property later this morning.'

'He has to be kidding! Did you tell him that I'm off now until after Christmas?'

'I told him that yesterday. Lisi, has something happened between you two?'

'Apart from the very obvious?' she asked tartly.

'You know what I mean.'

Yes, she knew what Marian meant and she guessed that it was pointless keeping it from her boss—especially as she had already guessed that Philip was Tim's father.

'I told him,' she said flatly.

'You *told* him?'

'He guessed,' Lisi amended.

'And?'

Lisi sighed. She had planned to get onto the phone first thing and tell Rachel all about it, but just then she badly needed to confide in somebody, and Marian was older and wiser. Lisi suspected that she had known straight away that a man as discerning as Philip would be bound to guess eventually.

'He wants to be involved.'

'With you?'

'Oh, no,' said Lisi with a hollow laugh. 'Definitely not with me. With Tim.'

'I see.' Marian's voice sounded rather strained. 'That explains it, then.'

That sense of foreboding hit her again. 'Explains what?' she asked, her voice rising with a kind of nameless fear.

'He really *does* want to buy somewhere here. In Langley.'

Lisi's mouth thinned. 'I see.'

'And that's not the worst of it.'

'What do you mean?'

'He wants *you* to show him around a property—'

'But I'm on *holiday*, Marian!'

'I already told him that.'

'And even if I weren't—I don't *want* to show him around a property!'

'He's…well, he's insisted, dear.'

'He can't insist,' whispered Lisi. 'Can he?'

Another pause. 'He *is* the customer,' said Marian apologetically, and suddenly Lisi understood. Marian was a businesswoman—and business was business was business. Philip Caprice was a wealthy and influential man and if he said jump, then presumably they would all have to leap through hoops for him.

She thought of all the times when Marian had let her have the morning, or even a couple of days, off work. When Tim had been ill. Or when she had taken him to have his inoculations. She was an understanding and kind employer, and Lisi owed her.

'Okay,' she sighed. 'I can probably arrange for Rachel to look after Tim. When does he want to look round?'

'Later on this morning. Think you can manage it? You can even leave Tim in here with us, if it's difficult.'

'I'm sure Rachel will be able to have him.'

'Good!' Marian's voice grew slightly more strained. 'There's just one more thing, Lisi.'

Lisi tried to inject a note of gallows humour into her voice. 'Go on, hit me with it!'

'The property in question…it's…it's The Old Rectory.'

The world spun. It was a cruel trick. A cruel twist of fate. Was he planning to hurt her even more than he already had done? Lisi heard herself speaking with a note of cracked desperation. 'Is this some kind of joke, Marian?'

'I wish it was, dear.'

Lisi didn't remember putting the phone down, she just found herself sitting on the bed staring blankly at it. He couldn't, she thought fiercely. He couldn't do this to her!

The Old Rectory.

The house she had grown up in. The house her mother had struggled to keep on, even after the death of her father, when everyone had told her to downsize and to move into something more suitable for a mother and her daughter on their own.

But neither of them had wanted to. A house could creep into your heart and your soul, and Lisi and her mother had preferred to put on an extra sweater or two in winter. It had kept the heating bills down at a time when every penny had counted.

After her mother had died, Lisi had reluctantly sold the house, but by then she had needed to. Really needed to, because she'd had a baby to support. She had bought Cherry Tree Cottage and invested the rest of the proceeds of the sale, giving just enough for her and Tim to live on. To fall back on.

And now Philip Caprice was going to rub her nose in it by buying the property for himself!

Over my dead body! she thought.

She gave Tim his breakfast.

'I want birthday cake,' he had announced solemnly.

'Sure,' said Lisi absently, and began to cut him a large slice.

'*Can* I, Mum-mee?' asked Tim, in surprise.

She glanced down at the sickly confection and remembered feeding Philip birthday cake all those years back and her heart clenched. She looked into Tim's hopeful face and relented. Oh, what the heck—it wouldn't hurt for once, would it?

While Tim was chomping his way through the cake, she phoned Rachel, who agreed to look after him without question.

'Bless you!' said Lisi impulsively.

'Is everything okay?'

She heard the doubt in Rachel's voice and wondered if she sounded as mixed-up and disturbed as she felt. Probably. 'I'll tell you all about it later,' she said grimly.

'Can't wait!'

Lisi went through the mechanics of getting ready. She ran herself a bath and left the door open and Tim trotted happily in and out. She wondered whether Philip was prepared for the lack of privacy which caring for a young child inevitably brought. And then she imagined him lording it in her old family home and she could have screamed aloud with fury, but for Tim's sake—and her own—she won the inner battle to stay calm.

She supposed that she ought to dress as if for work and picked out her most buttoned-up suit from the wardrobe. Navy-blue and pinstriped, it had a straight skirt which came to just below the knee and a long-line jacket. With a crisp, white blouse and her hair scraped back into a chignon, she thought that she looked professional. And prim.

Good!

The scarlet dress had been a big mistake last night. He might not like or respect her, but it was obvious that he still felt physically attracted to her. She had seen the way he'd watched her last night, while trying to appear as if he hadn't been. And she had seen the tension which had stiffened his elegant frame, had him shifting uncomfortably in his chair. It had been unmistakably a sexual tension, and Lisi wasn't fooling herself into thinking that it hadn't been mutual.

Later that morning, after she had deposited Tim and some of the leftover party food at Rachel's house, Lisi walked into the agency to find Philip waiting for her.

His face was unsmiling and his eyes looked very green as he nodded at her coolly. 'Hello, Lisi,' he said, speaking as politely and noncommittally—as if this were the first time he had ever met her.

Marian was sitting at her desk looking a little flustered. 'Here are the keys,' she said. 'The owners are away.'

Her heart sinking slightly, Lisi took them. She had hoped that one of the divorcing couple would be in. At least the presence of a third party might have defused the atmosphere. She could not think of a more unpalatable situation than being alone in that big, beautiful house with Philip.

Unpalatable? she asked herself. Or simply dangerous?

'We can walk there,' she told him outside. 'It's just up the lane.'

'Sure.'

But once away from Marian's view, she no longer had to play the professional. 'So you're going through with your threat to buy a house in the village,' she said, in a low, furious voice.

'I think it makes sense, under the circumstances,' he said evenly. 'Don't you?'

Nothing seemed to make sense any more—not least the fact that even in the midst of her anger towards him——her body was crying out for more of his touch.

Was that conditioning? Nature's way of ensuring stability? That a woman should find the father of her child overwhelmingly attractive? No. It couldn't be. Rachel had completely gone off Dave—she told Lisi that the thought of him touching her now made her flesh creep. But then Dave *had* run off with one of Rachel's other supposed 'friends'.

Lisi reminded herself that Philip was not whiter-than-white, either. *He* had been the one who had been attached—more than attached. He had actually been married, and yet his anger all seemed to be directed at her. His poor wife! It was, Lisi decided, time to start giving as good as she got.

Her rage was almost palpable, thought Philip as he looked at the stiff set of her shoulders beneath the starchy-looking suit she wore. He suspected that she had dressed in a way to make herself seem unapproachable and unattractive to him, but if that *had* been the case, then she had failed completely.

'This is in the same direction as *your* house,' he observed as she took him down the very route he had used last night.

She stopped dead in her tracks and gave h
questioning stare. 'You didn't know?'

'I've only seen the details.'

'It's just down the bloody *road* from me!'

'Handy,' he murmured.

She didn't want him making jokey little asides.
of comment could lull you into false hopes. She p
him hostile, she decided.

Her breath caught in her throat as they walked pa
cottage to the end of the lane, where, beside the old
Norman church, stood the beautiful old rectory. And
heart stood still with shock.

The place was practically falling down!

The yew hedge which her mother had always loving
clipped had been allowed to overgrow, and the lawn wa
badly in need of a cut.

'Not very well presented,' Philip observed.

'They're getting divorced,' explained Lisi icily. 'I don't
think that house-maintenance is uppermost in their minds
at the moment.'

He turned away. People sometimes said to him that death
must be easier to bear than divorce. When a couple divorced they knowingly ripped apart the whole fabric of
their lives. Only anger was left, and bitterness and resentment.

'At least Carla died knowing that you loved her, and she
loved you,' his mother had said to him softly after the fu-
neral and then, like now, he had turned away, his face a
mask of pain. What would his mother say if she knew how
he had betrayed that love?

And the woman who had tempted him stood beside him
now, mocking him and tempting him still in her prissy-
looking worksuit. He would be tied to Lisi for ever, he
realised—because children made a bond between two people which could never be broken.

Philip?' Her voice had softened, but that was instinctive
ther than intentional for she had seen the look of anguish
hich had darkened the carved beauty of his features.
hall we go inside, or did you want to look round the
arden first?'

He shook his head. 'Inside,' he said shortly.

Lisi had not been inside since the day when all the packing crates had made the faded old home resemble a ware-
house. She had perched on one waiting for the removals
van to arrive, her heart aching as she'd said goodbye to her
past. Tim had lain asleep in his Moses basket by her feet—
less than six months at the time—gloriously unaware of the
huge changes which had been taking place in his young
life.

Unbelievable to think that this was the first time she had
been back, but Marian had understood her reluctance to
accompany clients around her former home. Until Philip
Caprice had swanned into the office and made his autocratic
demand Lisi hadn't set foot inside the door.

Until today.

Lisi had to stifle a gasp.

When she had lived here with her mother there had been
very little money, but a whole lot of love. Surfaces had
been dusted, the floorboards bright and shiny, and there had
always been a large vase of foliage or the flowers which
had bloomed in such abundance in the large gardens at the
back.

But now the house had an air of neglect, as if no one
had bothered to pay any attention in caring for it. A
woman's tee shirt lay crumpled on one corner of the hall
floor and a half-empty coffee cup was making a sticky mark
on the window-ledge. Lisi shuddered as she caught the drift
of old cooking: onions or cabbage—something which lin-
gered unpleasantly in the unaired atmosphere.

She knew from statistics that most people decided to buy

a house within the first few seconds of walking into it. At least Philip was unlikely to be lured by this dusty old shell of a place. She thought of the least attractive way to view it, and she, above all others, knew the place's imperfections.

'The kitchen is along here,' she said calmly, and proceeded to take him there, praying that the divorcing couple had not had the funds to give the room the modernisation it had been crying out for.

She led the way in and let out an almost inaudible sigh of relief. Not only was the kitchen untouched, but it had clearly been left during some kind of marital dispute—for a smashed plate lay right in the centre of the floor. Pots and pans, some still containing food, lay on the surface of the hob, and there was a distinctly nasty smell emanating from the direction of the fridge.

He waited for her to make some kind of fumbling apology for the state of the place, but there was none, she just continued to regard him with that oddly frozen expression on her face.

'Like it?' she asked flippantly.

He narrowed his eyes. 'Hardly. Where's the dining room?'

'I'm afraid that it's some way from the kitchen,' she said, mock-apologetically. 'It isn't a terribly well-designed property—certainly not by modern standards.'

'You really don't want me to buy this house, do you, Lisi?'

'I don't want you to buy any house in Langley, if you must know.' And especially not this one. She put on her professional face once more. 'Would you like to see the dining room?'

'I can't wait,' he answered sardonically.

The dining room looked as though it had never had a meal eaten in it; instead there was a pile of legal-looking papers heaped up on the table, as if someone had been using it for a office. Philip looked around the room slowly, but said nothing.

'Where next?' asked Lisi brightly.

'To the next enchanting room,' he murmured.

Perversely, his criticism stung her, making her realise that she was still more attached to the place than she was sure she should be. How she wished he could have seen it when *she* had lived here, particularly at this time of the year. At Christmas it had come into its own. The hall used to be festooned with fresh laurel from the garden and stacks and stacks of holly and great sprigs of mistletoe had been bunched everywhere.

The choir would come from the church next door on Christmas Eve, and drink sherry and eat mince pies and the big, wide corridors would echo with the sound of excited chatter, while in the sitting room a log fire had blazed out its warmth.

Fortunately—or unfortunately in Lisi's case—no neglect could mar the beauty of the sitting room. The high ceiling and the carved marble fireplace drew the attention away from the fact that the curtains could have done with a good clean.

Philip nodded and walked slowly around the room, his eyes narrowing with pleasure as he looked out of the long window down into the garden beyond.

A winter-bare garden but beautiful nevertheless, he thought, with mature trees and bushes which were silhouetted against the curved shapes of the flower beds.

Lisi wandered over to the window and stood beside him, past and present becoming fused for one brief, poignant moment.

'You should see it in springtime,' she observed fondly.

He heard the dreamy quality of her voice which was so at odds with her attitude of earlier. 'Oh?'

'There are bulbs out everywhere—daffodils and tulips and narcissi—and over there…' she pointed to where a lone tree stood in the centre of the overgrown lawn '…underneath that cherry, the first snowdrops come out and the lawn is sprinkled with white, almost as if it had been snowing.'

The sense of something not being as it should be pricked at his senses. Instincts, Khalim had taught him. Always trust your instincts.

'You seem to know this house very well for someone who only works part-time in the estate agency,' he observed softly.

She turned to face him. What was the point of hiding it from him? 'You're very astute, Philip.'

'Just observant.' His dark brows winged upwards in arrogant query. 'So?'

'I used to live here.' No, that remark didn't seem to do the place justice. 'It was my childhood home,' she explained.

There she was, doing it again—that vulnerable little tremble of her mouth which made him want to kiss all her hurt away.

'What happened?' he asked abruptly.

'After my father died, it was just my mother and me—'

He sounded incredulous. 'In this great barn of a place?'

'We loved it,' she said simply.

He let his eyes roam once more over the high ceilings. 'Yes, I can see that you would,' he said slowly.

'We couldn't bear to leave it. When my mother died, I had to sell up, of course—because there was Tim to think about by then.'

'So you sold this and bought the cottage?' he guessed. 'And presumably banked the rest?'

She nodded.

He thought of her, all alone, struggling along with a little baby, and he felt the sharp pang of conscience. 'Lisi, why in God's name didn't you contact me? Even if I hadn't been able to offer you any kind of future—don't you think that I would have paid towards my son's upkeep?'

She gave him a look of icy pride. 'I wasn't going to come begging to you, cap in hand! I had to think of what was best for everyone, and I came to the conclusion that the best thing would be to cut all ties.'

'And did you enjoy playing God with people's lives?'

She heard his bitterness. 'I thought it would only complicate things if I tried to involve you—for you, for me, for Tim. And for your wife, of course,' she finished. 'Because if it had been me, and my husband had done what you did to her—it would have broken my heart.' She looked at him and her eyes felt hot with unshed tears for the dead woman she had unknowingly deceived. But not Philip—his betrayal had been cold-bloodedly executed. 'Did she know, Philip? Did your wife ever find out?'

'No,' he said flatly. 'Carla never knew anything about it.'

'Are you sure? They say that wives always know—only sometimes they pretend not to.' She stared at him as if she were seeing him for the first time. 'How could you do it? How could you do that to her and live with yourself afterwards?'

Her condemnation of him was so strong that he felt he could almost reach out and touch it, but he knew he couldn't let her stumble along this wrong track any longer, no matter how painful the cost of telling her.

'She didn't know,' he ground out, 'because she wasn't aware. Not of me, or you, or what happened. Not aware of anything.'

She blinked at him in confusion. 'What are you talking about?'

'The night I made love to you—my wife hadn't spoken to me for eighteen months.'

Foolish hope flared in her heart, putting an entirely different perspective on events. 'You mean...you mean that you were *separated*?'

He gave a bitter laugh at the unwitting irony of her words. 'In a sense, yes—we had been separated for a long time. You see, the car crash happened *before* I met you, Lisi, not after. It left her in a deep coma from which she never recovered. She didn't die for several months after...after...'

'After what?' she whispered.

His eyes grew even bleaker. 'After I made love to you. You must have been about six months pregnant when she died.'

CHAPTER SEVEN

THE sitting-room of her childhood retreated into a hazy blur and then came back into focus again and Lisi stared at Philip, noting the tension which had scored deep lines down the side of his mouth.

'I don't understand,' she said.

'Don't you?' He gave a short laugh. 'My wife—'

His wife. His *wife*. 'What was her name?'

He hesitated, then frowned. What was it to her? 'Carla,' he said, grudgingly.

Carla. A person who was referred to as a 'wife' was a nebulous figure of no real substance, but Carla—Carla existed. Philip's wife. Carla. It hurt more than it had any right to hurt. 'Tell me,' she urged softly.

He wasn't looking for her sympathy, or her understanding—he would give her facts if she wanted to hear them, but he wanted nothing in return.

'It happened early one autumn morning,' he began, and a tale he had not had to recount for such a long time became painfully alive in his mind as he relived it. 'Carla was driving to work. She worked out of London,' he added, as if that somehow mattered. 'And visibility was poor. There were all the usual warnings on the radio for people to take it easy, but cars were driving faster than they should have done. A lorry ran into the back of her.' He paused, swallowing down the residual rage that people were always in a hurry and stupid enough to ignore the kind of conditions which led to accidents.

'When the paramedics arrived on the scene, they didn't think she'd make it. She had suffered massive head injuries.

They took her to hospital, and for a while it was touch and go.'

Lisi winced. What words could she say that would not sound meaningless and redundant? He must have heard the same faltering platitudes over and over again. She nodded and said nothing.

'Her body was unscathed,' he said haltingly. 'And so was her face—that was the amazing thing.' But it had been a cruel paradox that while she had lain looking so perfect in the stark hospital bed—the Carla he had known and loved had no longer existed. Smashed away by man's disregard for safety.

'I used to visit her every day—twice a day when I wasn't out of London.' Sitting there for hours, playing her favourite music, stroking the cold, unmoving hand and praying for some kind of response, some kind of recognition he was never to see again. Other than one slight movement of her fingers which had given everyone false hope. 'But she was so badly injured. She couldn't speak or eat, or even breathe for herself.'

'How terrible,' breathed Lisi, and in that moment her heart went out to him.

'The doctors weren't even sure whether she could hear me, but I talked to her anyway. Just in case.'

He met a bright kind of understanding in her eyes and he hardened his heart against it. 'I was living in a kind of vacuum,' he said heavily. 'And work became my salvation, in a way.' At work he had been forced to put on hold the human tragedy which had been playing non-stop in his life. He gave her a hard, candid look. 'Women came onto me all the time, but I was never...'

She sensed what was coming. 'Never what, Philip?'

'Never tempted,' he snarled. 'Never.' His mouth hardened. 'Until you.'

So she *was* the scapegoat, was she? Was that why he

had seemed so *angry* when he had walked back into her life? 'You make me sound like some kind of *femme fatale*,' she said drily.

He shook his head. That had been his big mistake. A complete misjudgement. Uncharacteristic, but understandable under the circumstances. 'On the contrary,' he countered. 'You seemed the very opposite of a *femme fatale*. I thought that you were sweet, and safe. Innocent. Uncomplicated.'

Achingly, she noted his use of the past tense.

'Until that night. When we had that celebratory drink.' He walked back over to the window and stared out unseeingly. 'I'd only had one drink myself—so I couldn't even blame the alcohol.'

Blame. He needed someone to blame—and she guessed that someone was her. 'So I was responsible for your momentary weakness, was I, Philip?'

He turned around and his face was a blaze of anger. 'Do you make a habit of getting half-cut and borrowing men's hotel rooms to sleep it off?' he ground out, because this had been on his mind for longer than he cared to remember. 'Do you often take off all your clothes and lie there, just waiting, like every man's fantasy about to happen?'

'Is that what you think?' she asked quietly, even though her heart was crashing against her ribcage.

'I'm not going to flatter myself that I was the first,' he said coldly. 'Why should I? You didn't act like it was a once-in-a-lifetime experience.'

His words wounded her—but what defence did she have? If she told him that it had *felt* like that, for her, then she would come over at best naive, and at worst—a complete and utter liar.

'I'll take that as a compliment,' she said, and regretted it immediately. 'I'm sorry,' she amended. 'I shouldn't be flippant when you're telling me all this.'

Oddly enough, her glib remark did not offend him. 'It was a long time ago,' he said heavily. 'I don't want to be wrapped up in cotton wool for the rest of my life.'

'Won't you tell me the rest?' she asked slowly, because she recognised that he was not just going to go away. And if he *was* around in her life—then how could they possibly form any kind of relationship to accommodate their son, unless she knew all the facts? However painful they might be.

He nodded. 'That night I left you I went straight to the hospital. The day before Carla had moved her fingers slightly and it seemed as if there might be hope.'

She remembered that his mood that day had been almost high. So that had been why. His wife had appeared to be on the road to recovery and he had celebrated life in the oldest way known to man. With her.

'But Carla lay as still as ever, hooked up to all the hospital paraphernalia of tubes and drips and monitors,' he continued.

He had sat beside her and been eaten up with guilt and blame and regret as he'd looked down at her beautiful but waxy lips which had breathed only with the aid of a machine. Carla hadn't recognised him, or had any idea of what he had done, and yet it had smitten him to the hilt that he had just betrayed his wife in the most fundamental way possible.

His mouth twisted. To love and to cherish. In sickness and in health. Vows he had made and vows he had broken.

He had always considered himself strong, and reasoned and controlled—and the weakness which Lisi had exposed in his character had come as an unwelcome shock to which had made him despise himself.

And a little bit of him had despised her, too.

'She died a few months later,' he finished, because what else was there to say? He saw her stricken expression and guessed what had caused it. 'Oh, it wasn't as a result of what you and I did, Lisi, if that's what you're thinking.'

'The thought had crossed my mind,' she admitted slowly. 'Even though I know it's irrational.'

Hadn't he thought the same thing himself? As though Carla could have somehow known what he had done.

'What did you do?' she questioned softly.

There was silence in the big room before he spoke again.

'I went to pieces, I guess.' He saw the look of surprise in her eyes. 'Oh, I functioned as before—I worked and I ate and I slept—but it was almost as if it was happening to another person. I think I was slowly going crazy. And then Khalim came.'

'Khalim?' she asked hesitantly.

'Prince Khalim.' He watched as the surprise became astonishment, and he shrugged. 'At the time he was heir to a Middle-Eastern country named Maraban—though of course he's ruler now.'

'How do you know him?' asked Lisi faintly.

'We were at Cambridge together—and he heard what had happened and he came and took me off to Maraban with him.'

'To live in luxury?'

He smiled at *this* memory as he shook his head. 'The very opposite. He told me that the only way to live through pain and survive it was to embrace it. So for two months we lived in a tiny hut in the Maraban mountains. Just us. No servants. Nothing. Just a couple of discreet bodyguards lurking within assassination distance of him.'

Her eyes grew wide with fascination. 'And what did you do?'

'We foraged for food. We walked for hours and sometimes rode horses through the mountains. At night we would read by the light of the fire. And he taught me to fight,' he finished.

'To *fight*?'

He nodded. 'Bare-knuckled. We used to beat hell out of each other!'

'And didn't he...*mind*?'

Philip shook his head. 'Out there, in the mountains—we were equals.' Indeed, he suspected that Khalim had learned as much from the experience as he had—for certainly the two men who had emerged from their self-imposed exile had been changed men.

She had wondered what had brought about the new, lean, hard Philip. Why he had looked so different—all the edges chiselled away. She swallowed. 'And then?'

'Then he offered me a job, working as his emissary. It took me all over the world.'

'And did you enjoy it?'

'I loved it.'

'But you left?'

He nodded.

'Why?'

'The time had come. Everything has its time of closure. Khalim fell in love with an English woman. Rose.'

His mouth curved into a warm and affectionate smile and Lisi felt the dagger of jealousy ripping through her.

'Khalim and I had developed the closeness of brothers— in so much as his position allowed. It was only right that Rose should have him all to herself once they were married.'

In all the time she had been listening to his story, Lisi had been entranced, but as he drew to the end of it reality reared its head once more.

She gave a little cough. 'Would you like to see upstairs now?'

'No, thanks—I've seen enough.'

Thank God! She nodded understandingly. 'Well, I'm sure

we'll be getting a lot more properties on the market—especially after Christmas.'

He gave a slow smile as he realised what she was thinking. 'You may have misunderstood me, Lisi,' he said silkily. 'I want this house and I want you to put an offer in.'

'But it's overpriced! You know it is!' she declared desperately. 'Ridiculously overpriced!'

He wondered whether she tried to put *other* buyers off in quite such an obvious way, but somehow doubted it. 'So Marian Reece told me.'

'And they've stated *unequivocally* that they can't possibly accept anything other than the full asking price.'

'Then offer it to them,' he said flatly.

She could not believe her ears. This was Philip Caprice speaking—the man famed for driving the hardest bargain in the property market! 'Are you serious?' she breathed.

He saw the way her lips parted in disbelief and he felt a wild urge to kiss them, to imprison her in his arms and to take the clips from her hair and have it tumble down over that masculine-looking jacket. His eyes slid down past the pencil skirt to the creamy tights which covered her long legs and that same wildness made him wonder what she would do if he began to make love to her.

Should he try? See if she would respond with passion and let him slide his hand all the way up her legs and touch her until she was begging him for more. He struggled to dampen down his desire.

'I've never been more serious in my life,' he said, and then his voice became clipped. 'Tell the vendors that my only condition is that I want *in* and I want them out. So let's tie up the deal as quickly as possible, shall we?'

If she could have had a wish at that moment, it would have been to have been given a huge sum of money—enough to buy back her own home herself instead of letting it go to Philip Caprice. Couldn't he guess how much she loved the place? Wasn't he perceptive enough to realise how heartbreaking she was going to find it, with *him* living here.

Or maybe he just didn't care.

He was walking around the room now, touching the walls with a proprietorial air she found utterly abhorrent. She gritted her teeth behind a forced smile. 'Very well. I'll get that up and running straight away.' There was a question in her eyes. 'Though it's going to need a lot of work to get it up to the kind of specifications I imagine you'll be looking for.'

His answering smile was bland. 'Just so.'

'You certainly couldn't expect to be in before Christmas. Probably not until springtime at the earliest,' she added hopefully.

Her wishes were beautifully transparent, but, unfortunately for her, they were not going to come true. 'Not Christmas, certainly,' he agreed, and saw her visibly relax. 'But I think spring is a rather pessimistic projection.'

'All the builders and decorators around here are booked up for *months* in advance!' she told him, trying to keep the note of triumph from her voice.

'Then I shall just have to bring people down from London, won't I?'

She glared at him. 'As you wish,' she said tightly. 'And now, if there's nothing further, I'll call into the office and then I really must get back—'

'To Tim?' he interjected softly.

How she wished he wouldn't use that distinctly possessive tone! He might be Tim's father—but the two had barely exchanged a few words. He couldn't just walk back into their lives unannounced and expect to be an equal partner!

'Yes, to Tim,' she said coldly, and began to walk towards

the hall, her high heels clip-clopping over the polished floorboards.

'Oh, Lisi?'

She stopped, something in his tone warning her that she was not going to like his *next* words, either. She turned round, wishing that he were ugly, and that he didn't have those piercing green eyes which could turn her knees to jelly. 'Yes?'

'We haven't discussed Christmas yet, have we?'

'Christmas?' she echoed stupidly. 'What about it?'

'I want to spend it with Tim.'

She fought down the urge to tell him that he could take a running jump, but she knew that open opposition would get her nowhere. Softly, softly it must be.

She put on her most reasonable smile. 'I'm afraid you can't. I'm really sorry.'

Yeah, she sounded *really* sorry. He kept his face impassive. 'Oh? And why's that?'

'Because we've already made arrangements for Christmas.'

'Then unmake them,' he said flatly. 'Or include me.'

She drew in a deep breath. 'We've arranged to have lunch with my friend Rachel and her son, Blaine—he's Tim's best friend. I couldn't possibly take you along with us!'

He thought about it. 'I'm supposed to be having lunch with my parents,' he reflected. 'But I'll drive down here afterwards. We can all have tea and Christmas cake together, can't we, Lisi?'

'*No!*'

'Why not?'

'Because…because he doesn't know who you are!'

He narrowed his eyes, but not before she had seen the flash of temper in them. 'You mean you haven't told him yet?'

'When?' she demanded angrily. 'In the hour I had this morning between waking up and being summoned into the office at your bidding?'

The accusation washed over him. 'I thought that it was important for you to see where I was buying.'

'*Why?*'

'Because eventually Tim will come to stay with me. Naturally.'

Feeling as though her world were splintering all around her, Lisi prayed that it didn't show. Keep calm, she told herself. He may be powerful and rich, but he can't just ride roughshod over your wishes. He can't.

She drew a deep breath.

'Listen, Philip—I can understand that you want to build a relationship with Tim—'

'How very good of you,' he put in sarcastically.

'But he doesn't know you properly, and until he does then I'm afraid that I cannot permit him to stay with you. In fact, he probably won't want to come up to the house without me.'

The expression on his face grew intent. 'I want bathtimes and bedtimes and all the normal things which fathers do, and if you think I'm cracking my skull on the ceiling of your cottage every time I stand up, then you've got another think coming!'

She opened her mouth to object and then shut it again, because she could see from his unshakable stance that to argue would be pointless. 'I can't see that happening for a long time,' she said coldly.

'We'll see.' He gave a bland smile. 'And in the meantime, I'll be around on Christmas afternoon. Shall we say around five?'

She couldn't bring herself to answer him, and so she nodded instead.

CHAPTER EIGHT

'TIM, darling—*please* don't eat any more—you'll be sick!'

'*One* more, Mum-mee!'

Lisi lunged towards him, but he had crammed another chocolate in his mouth before she could stop him. She took the stocking away from him firmly. 'That's enough chocolate!' she said sternly. 'We've got tea to get through next.' And her face fell.

Rachel leaned across the table, holding a bottle of port. 'Have a glass?' she suggested. 'You haven't got far to go, and it *is* Christmas Day!'

'You don't need to remind me,' said Lisi gloomily. She looked down at her son, who was busy licking chocolate off the inside of the wrapper. 'Put that down, darling, and go away and play with Blaine until it's time to go!'

To her relief, Tim went scampering off, and, after a swift glance at her wrist-watch, Lisi curled her feet up underneath her. Another hour until the avenging Caprice appeared on her doorstep. 'I could just go to sleep.' She yawned.

'On Christmas Day? Show me the mother of a child under ten who couldn't, and I'll show you a liar!' chortled Rachel, and then a look of concern criss-crossed her brow as she glanced across at her friend. 'You okay?'

Lisi shrugged. 'As okay as anyone can be when they're having their arm twisted.' She had told Rachel everything. She had seen no cause not to. There was no longer any point in keeping anything back. People would know—or guess—soon enough when she and Tim started traipsing down the lane for cosy afternoons and evenings with him!

'I still can't believe he's bought The Old Rectory,' said

Lisi crossly. 'And what is even more unbelievable is that he railroaded his lawyers into rushing through the deal. They complete in the New Year,' she finished. 'What a wonderful way to start the year—Philip Caprice firmly ensconced in my old family home.'

'I think it's rather romantic,' sighed Rachel.

'Romantic?' squeaked Lisi.

'Mmm. I can't imagine Dave doing something like that—even if he could afford to.'

'But you wouldn't want him to, would you?' asked Lisi, raising her eyebrows in surprise. 'I thought you said that if you never saw him again, it would be much too soon?'

Rachel shrugged and swirled her port around in the glass, so that it looked like a claret-coloured whirlpool. 'I suppose not. It's just that sometimes I get lonely—well, often, actually—and Christmas is the worst. Even if Dave wasn't the most wonderful husband in the world, at least he was *there*. I guess I miss having a man around the place.'

And that was the difference between them, thought Lisi—she had been content enough with her single status. Not that she had been anti-men, or anything like that—she just hadn't particularly missed having a partner. Until she reminded herself that she had never actually *had* a partner.

'I'd better think about making a move,' she said reluctantly, thinking how warm and cosy it was by Rachel's fireside.

Rachel nodded. 'You'll need to change.'

'Will I hell? There's nothing wrong with this dress!'

'Except that Tim has smeared chocolate all over it,' commented Rachel, with a smile.

Lisi looked down at her dress to see several brown, sticky thumbprints! She smiled at her friend. 'We've had a wonderful time today,' she said softly.

'Me, too.'

'Sure you won't come over for a drink later on?'

Rachel pulled a face and giggled. 'And face the daunting Philip Caprice after what you've told me about him? Er, I'll take a rain check, thanks, Lisi!'

Lisi packed up their presents in a carrier bag and wrapped Tim up warmly in his little duffle-coat and the brand-new bobble hat and matching scarf which Santa had brought him. She kissed Rachel and Blaine goodbye and they set off home in the crisp air.

Although it was only just past four, it was already pitch-black and there was a curious silence which had descended over the whole village. But then it *was* Christmas Day. Everyone was inside, making merry with their families—falling asleep after their big lunches, or playing games or watching weepie films on television.

She let them in and thought how cold the house was. Better light a fire. She drew the curtains and knelt in front of the brand-new toy railway track and began to push one of the trucks around it with her finger. 'Choo-choo,' she chanted. 'Choo-choo!'

'*Me*, Mum-mee! Me play with the train!'

She smiled. 'Go on, then, and I'll light the fire.'

She efficiently dealt with the logs and paper until the blaze was spitting and glowing. She put the big fire-guard in front of it, and went into her bedroom to change.

She had just stripped off her dress and was standing in her bra and pants when there was a knock at the front door and she glanced at her watch in horror. He couldn't be here! Not yet. But who else would it be on Christmas afternoon?

Saying a few choice words underneath her breath, she dragged on her dressing gown and opened the front door to find his tall figure dominating her view, blotting out the moon completely. He was carrying presents, but she barely gave them a second glance. Not only had he demanded this visit—he didn't even have the courtesy to be on time!

'You're early!' she accused.

He thought that no woman had the right to look as sexy as that—not when she was wearing an old flannelette dressing gown which had clearly seen better days—but Lisi did. Maybe it was something to do with the fact that he knew only too well what fabulous curves lay beneath its rather shapeless covering. Or because, for once, she had let her hair fall free and unfettered, spilling in abundant ebony streams to her waist. He had only ever seen it loose once before and he felt the blood begin to sing in his veins as he remembered just when.

'And a very happy Christmas to you, too,' he replied sardonically. 'I left my parents slightly ahead of schedule because they predicted snow—'

'Where?' asked Lisi, theatrically peering at the sky and then at the ground. 'I don't see any snow!'

He tried to take into consideration the fact that she had obviously been changing. 'My apologies,' he murmured. 'And now, do you think I can come inside? It's getting pretty chilly standing here.'

She held the door open ungraciously, but as she closed it on the bitter night she reminded herself that she had vowed there would be no unpleasantness. Not in front of Tim. And especially not today, of all days.

Philip lowered his voice. 'Have you told him?'

She bit her lip. 'Not yet.'

He looked at her in disbelief. 'Hell, Lisi—it's been a week!'

She shook her head. 'I just couldn't work out how to do it—it's not something you can come out with very easily and explain to a child of three. ''By the way, darling—you know that strange man who turned up on the doorstep on your birthday? Well, he's your daddy!'''

'There's no need to make it sound so—'

'So like the truth?'

He sighed. 'So when *are* you going to tell him?'

'Not *me*, Philip. Us. You, mainly.'

'*Me?*'

'Yes, you! I'll leave you to do the talking—I'm sure you'll put it in the most diplomatic way possible.' Hot tears stung at her eyes and she turned away before he could see them. 'I just haven't got a clue what to say. *Tim!*' she called. 'Tim!'

'Is it Faver Chrissmas 'gain?' squeaked a little voice and Tim came pelting out and almost collided with the tall figure in the hall. He looked up at him with huge aquamarine eyes.

So like Lisi's eyes, thought Philip. 'Hello,' he said.

'You're Mum-mee's friend!' announced Tim triumphantly.

'That's right! And I've come to have tea with you both— if that's okay with you?'

'Did Faver Chrissmas bring you lots of presents?'

'Not lots,' said Philip gravely. 'Some.'

'I got lots!'

Philip smiled. 'Do you want to show me?'

Tim nodded excitedly and eyed the brightly wrapped parcels in Philip's arms with interest. 'Who are *those* presents for?' he asked coyly.

Philip laughed. 'They're for you. We'll open them when Mummy has changed out of her dressing gown.' He shot Lisi a questioning look and she realised that she had been standing there just gawping.

'I'll go and get changed.' She nodded, wondering just how he had always had the knack of seeming to be in charge!

She shut the bedroom door behind her, her heart thundering just with the knowledge that *he* was here, such a short distance away, and that she was standing in her underwear and looking at it critically in the mirror.

A functional peach-coloured bra and knickers which

didn't even match—but who cared? She certainly wasn't planning for him to get a glimpse of them.

But you would like him to, wouldn't you? taunted a mischievous voice in her head, and she shook her head at her reflection in the mirror.

She still wanted him, yes—but things were complicated enough as they were. Resuming a physical relationship with him would only add to those. She gave a wry smile as she pulled on a pair of old blue jeans and an ice-blue sweater. Who was she kidding? As if a few short hours in someone's arm could be defined as a relationship.

She raked the brush through her hair, tempted to tie it back—but decided that she couldn't leave him sitting out there waiting for her for much longer, so she left it loose.

She walked back into the sitting room to find that he was playing trains with Tim, and when he looked up his eyes were quietly smouldering.

'Is—everything okay?' she asked.

He steeled himself against the impact of her beauty, and jerked his head towards the roaring fire instead. He stood up and came to stand beside her, lowering his voice into an undertone so that only she could hear. 'Do you usually leave Tim here on his own, while you titillate yourself in the next room?'

For a moment she didn't quite get his drift, and when she did her mouth set itself into a mulish line. So he thought he could walk back into their lives and start criticising her skills as a mother, did he?

'I was hardly titillating,' she answered icily, gesturing to her casual clothes with an angry, jerking motion. 'Just getting changed out of a dress which Tim had liberally smeared with chocolate.'

'Lisi, he was alone in the room with a fire—for heaven's sake! Do you really think that's safe for a three-year-old?'

The injustice of it stung her. 'I'll go and put the kettle

on,' she said, between gritted teeth, and marched out to the kitchen.

He followed her, as she had known he would, but remained standing in the doorway so that he could keep an eye on the toddler who was still engrossed in his new train-set.

He saw the fury in the stiff set of her shoulders. 'Listen, I wasn't meaning to be judgemental,' he said softly.

She clicked the kettle on and turned round, her eyes spitting pale blue fire. 'Like hell you weren't!'

'I was only just pointing out—'

'Well, don't!' she said, in a low, shaking voice. 'Do you think I've brought him up in a house which has a fire and not taught him that he is never to go near it?'

'Listen—'

'No, *you* listen! What do you think it's like as a single parent living with a little boy? Have you ever stopped to think about it?'

'Actually, no—but then it wasn't number one on my list of priorities. Until now.'

She met the quizzical green stare fearlessly. 'Even taking a bath has to be planned with all the attention you would give to a military campaign!' she declared. 'As for going to the bathroom—well, you don't want to know!'

He glanced back towards Tim and then at her again. It had never occurred to him. Why should it? People rarely considered the practical problems of child-rearing unless they were contemplating taking the plunge themselves. He sighed. 'You're right. I had no right—'

'No, you didn't!' she agreed furiously. 'You have only to take a look at him to realise that he is a happy, contented little boy. The world is full of dangers, Philip—and I have had to teach him about them all. Never to talk to strangers. Never to approach a dog that might bite him. The fact that the roads aren't safe—' She saw him flinch, and wished she hadn't chosen an example which would remind him of Carla. 'I'm sorry.'

He shook his head. 'The cotton-wool remark still holds true. I shouldn't have said what I did.'

'No, you shouldn't!' She pointed to the kitchen cupboards with an air of frustration. 'I've had all these cupboards child-proofed so that he can't get into them. I don't leave bottles of bleach lying around the place for him to find—and there's a stair-gate at the foot of the stairs! Please credit me with a little more sense and caring, Philip! He has had it drummed into him from the word go that fires are dangerous and must be treated with respect and caution—and that Mummy is the only person who touches the fire.'

He watched her warm the pot and then make the tea. He had been lucky in a way, he guessed. She could have been the kind of mother who didn't care—who saw Tim as a mistake who had taken away her youth and her freedom. But she had created a home for him, a warm and loving home, he realised.

She was right. You had only to look at the child to see that he was happy and contented and well cared for. Stimulated, too—to judge from his conversation.

'Can I do anything?' he asked.

She couldn't resist it. 'Better go back in and keep your eye on Tim,' she said sweetly. 'I can manage here.'

He nodded, and his gaze swept over her, beguiling her and capturing her in its intense green light. 'And we'll tell him?'

Lisi swallowed. She couldn't keep putting it off. *They* couldn't keep putting it off. 'I have no choice, do I?' she asked quietly, but noticed that he didn't bother answering that—he didn't need to—just turned away and walked back into the sitting room.

She carried the tea-tray through and brought in Christmas cake and mince pies and slices of Stollen.

Philip looked up as she began to unload it all onto the table and gave a rueful smile. 'Not sure if I can eat again— at least until the New Year.'

She forced herself to be conversational. They were shortly to drop the biggest bombshell into Tim's life—let him see that his mother and his father didn't actually hate one another.

'Did your mother feed you up?'

He nodded. 'It's my first Christmas here for years—in Maraban they don't celebrate it.'

Tim looked up. 'Where's Malaban?' he chirped.

'Maraban,' corrected Philip, and his eyes softened as he looked down at the interested face of his son. 'It's a country in the Middle East. A beautiful land with a great big desert—do you know what a desert is, Tim?'

He shook his dark head, mesmerised.

'It's made of sand—lots of sand—and only the very toughest of plants can grow there.'

'What telse?' asked Tim. 'In Malaban?'

Philip smiled. 'Oh, there are fig trees and wild walnut trees, and the mountain slopes are covered in forests of juniper and pistachio trees—'

'What's st-stachio tree?' piped up Tim. 'Like an apple tree?'

Philip shook his head. 'Not really. A pistachio is a nut,' he explained. 'A delicious pale green nut in a little shell—'

'He's too young for nuts!' put in Lisi immediately.

He guessed that he deserved that, and nodded. 'Oh, and there are lots of animals there, too,' he said. 'Jackals and wild boar and rare, pink deer.'

Tim's eyes were like saucers, thought Lisi. He probably thought that Philip was concocting a wonderful fairy-tale land, and, come to think of it, that was exactly what it sounded like.

'Do you live there?' asked Tim.

'I did. But not any more.'

'Why?'

'Because it was time for me to come back to England.'

'Why?'

'Tim—' began Lisi, but Philip shook his head.

'I used to work for a prince.'

Lisi looked at Tim—now he really *did* think that this was a story!

'A *real* prince?'

'Uh-huh. Prince Khalim. Only the prince got married and so it was time for me to move on.'

Tim nodded solemnly. 'Will you play trains with me?'

He met her eyes across the room. *Now*, they urged her, and Lisi knew that she must begin this particular story. She took time pouring tea, and gave Tim a beaker of juice, and then she went to sit down on the floor next to both of them and cleared her throat.

'Tim, darling?'

A train was chugged along the track by a small, chubby finger.

'Tim? Look at Mummy, darling.'

His long-lashed eyes locked on hers and she felt the almost painfully overwhelming love of motherhood. She steadied her breathing. 'Do you remember that once you asked me why you hadn't got a daddy?'

Philip stilled as Tim nodded.

'And I told you that he had gone away a long time ago and that I wasn't sure if he was ever coming back?'

Again Tim nodded, but this time Philip flinched.

'Well…' She hesitated, but in her heart she knew that there was no way to say this other than using clear and truthful words which a three-year-old would understand. 'Well, he did come back, darling and…'

Tim was staring up at Philip. 'Are *you* my daddy?'

He felt the prick of tears at the back of his eyes as he nodded. 'Yes, Tim,' he answered, his voice thickening. 'I am.'

Tim nodded, and bent his head to push the train around the track once more.

'Tim?' questioned Lisi tentatively, because she couldn't see the expression on his face, and when he lifted it it was unusually calm and accepting, as if he were told things like this every day of the week.

'An' are you going 'way again? To Malaban?' he asked casually, as if it didn't really matter, but Lisi could tell from that oddly fierce look of concentration on his little face that it did.

Philip shook his head, unable to speak for a moment. 'No, Tim,' he said eventually. 'I'm not going anywhere. I'm going to buy a house in the village and see you as many weekends as your mummy will let me.'

He met her gaze with a question in his eyes.

So if I don't let him, then I'm the big, bad witch, she thought bitterly.

'An' are you and Mummy getting married?'

The silence which greeted this remark made Lisi as uncomfortable as she had ever felt in her life. She shook her head. 'Oh, no, darling—nothing like that!'

'Why?'

Oh, *why* had she brought him up to be so alert and questioning? To pursue every subject until he was satisfied with the answers?

'Because not all mummies and daddies live together, now, do they?' she asked gently. 'Blaine's daddy doesn't live with Blaine's mummy any more, does he?'

'That's 'cos he's livin' with a witch!'

'A *witch*?' squeaked Lisi in confusion.

'That's what Blaine heard his Mum-mee say!'

Philip bit back a smile. He suspected that the word had been 'bitch'. 'I would like to get to know you a little better, if that's okay with you, Tim. And Mummy and I will be great friends, won't we, Lisi?'

'Oh, yes,' she agreed, but her eyes flashed him a different message entirely. 'Definitely.'

'So what have you got to say to all that?' asked Philip, and, unable to resist it for any longer, reached out his hand to ruffle the silky blackness of the little head.

Tim put his train down and looked up at her. 'Can I have more chocolate, Mum-mee?' he asked.

The question shattered the tension in the atmosphere, and Philip and Lisi both burst out laughing, their eyes colliding in a brief expression of shared joy that made her heart thunder beneath her breast. It's just relief, she told herself fiercely—nothing to do with her. Tim has accepted him, and he's got what he wanted.

Though she wouldn't have been human if she hadn't half hoped that he wouldn't.

She put more logs on the fire and then watched while Philip wholeheartedly entered into playing with Tim. For a man with little or no experience of children, she was forced to the conclusion that he was very good with them. If Tim's reaction was anything to go by.

He stared wide-eyed while Philip made a horse out of some balloons and then blew up some others and let the air whizz out of them in a sound which had Tim collapsing in peals of giggles.

She had taken all the remains of the tea back out to the kitchen, and when she returned it was to find them playing rough and tumble on the rug and she realised that there were some things that fathers could do, which mothers never could.

They both looked up as she walked in, both flushed with pleasure but tinged with a kind of guilt—identical expressions on their faces. How could I ever have thought that they weren't alike? thought Lisi with a touch of despair. The colouring might be hers, but Marian was right: he *did* have bits of Philip—lots of Philip—in him. Of course he did.

Gently, Philip lowered Tim back down onto the carpet, from where he had been sitting on his shoulders, and stood up.

'Am I interrupting your routine, Lisi?'

So I am the bringer of routine and order, and he provides the fun, does he? thought Lisi. Or was she being unfair?

Philip saw the look of discomfort which had pleated her brow and understood exactly what had caused it. She had agreed to let him get to know Tim, but she had probably not anticipated what a success it would be.

Neither had he.

A different child might have refused to answer him. Or spoken in sulky monosyllables. Not chatted so openly and with such obvious interest. And much of that must be down to her.

'It's your bathtime, Tim,' she said, with a quick glance at her watch, and then forced herself to meet Philip's gaze. 'Unless you'd like to?'

He would like to. He wanted to bath his son more than he had wanted anything in a long time, but he recognised that Lisi might now be feeling the outsider. He shook his head. 'No, you do it. He's used to you.'

'Philip do it!' demanded Tim, unwilling to lose sight of his new friend.

Philip shook his head. 'I have to make a few phone calls,' he said.

She carried Tim to the bathroom and wondered who he was phoning on Christmas Day. Obviously somebody very close to him. He had told her that he wasn't married—but that didn't preclude a girlfriend, did it?

But he kissed you, a voice reminded her. He kissed you passionately and told you that he still wanted you—would he betray a second woman if he got the opportunity?

He isn't going to *get* the opportunity, she told herself as she squirted bubble bath into the running water and watched it become big, foamy clouds. No matter how much *she* wanted to—it wasn't right. There was too much bitter history behind them and only potential heartache lay ahead if she was crazy enough to give in.

She let Tim splash around in the bath for ages, wondering whether Philip would stick around. He might just get the message and go. But he was still there, talking in a low voice into his mobile phone as she carried a sleepy, pyjama-clad Tim past the sitting room to his bedroom and tenderly put him into bed.

'Have you had a lovely Christmas, darling?' she asked him softly.

'Yes, Mum-mee.' His eyes opened wide. 'Is Philip coming tomorrow?'

She sincerely hoped not, but she made herself smile a placating smile. 'We'll see. Okay?'

He nodded against the pillow, letting his eyelids drift down, and then automatically stuck his thumb in his mouth.

He was almost asleep, but story-telling was sacrosanct and Lisi put her hand out and pulled out the nearest book, which just happened to be *Cinderella*. How very appropriate, she thought wryly, and began to read.

She waited until she was certain that he was sound asleep, then reluctantly made her way back to where Philip lay sprawled on the floor in front of the fire, his phone-call finished. He had, she noted with surprise, put all the toys neatly away, so that the room for once didn't look as though a bomb had hit it. She had never had anyone do that for her before.

She hovered in the doorway, unsure of what to say or do. She could hardly ask him to leave. 'Can I get you a drink of something?'

He heard the lack of enthusiasm in her voice. 'One for the road?' he suggested sardonically.

She shrugged. 'If you like.'

He shook his head, got to his feet and went over to where she stood. 'No, thanks. You must be tired.'

Again she had the sense of him dominating the room, of his raw masculinity exuding from every pore of that spectacular body. In an effort to distract herself, she said, rather awkwardly, 'It went well, I think, didn't it?'

'Yes.' He was aching to touch her, but he realised that he owed her something. 'Thank you, Lisi,' he said simply. 'For letting me.'

She wasn't going to read anything into what he said. This was a purely practical arrangement, solely for the welfare of Tim. 'I had no choice, did I?' she questioned tartly. 'I imagine that if I'd refused you would have sought some kind of legal redress.'

Her brittle words extinguished the warmth he had been feeling, but did absolutely nothing to put out the fire in his groin. He knew he shouldn't do this, but something drove him on—a need to see that cold, frozen look wiped clean off her beautiful face.

He reached his hand out to cup her chin, his thumb and his forefinger stroking along its outline almost reflectively.

Lisi shivered. Where he touched her, he set her on fire. She knew that she should move away but something was stopping her and she wasn't sure what. 'Please don't,' she whispered.

Her lacklustre words belied the shining darkness in her

eyes and the need to kiss her overpowered him. 'You want me to,' he whispered back.

'No—'

But he kissed the word away with his mouth, feeling its unresisting softness become as hard and as urgent as his.

She rocked against him—all the cold and the hunger and frustration she had experienced letting itself go as his mouth explored hers with a thoroughness guaranteed to set her on the path to inevitable seduction. She felt the prickling sensation as her breasts grew heavy and aroused, and a long-forgotten molten sweetness began to build up at the very core of her.

Her mind was spinning. She wanted to burrow her hands up beneath his sweater and to feel the warm bare silk of his skin once more, but she had been a mother for too long to let her own wishes be paramount. For one split-second she imagined what could—*would*—happen next, if she didn't put a stop to it.

They couldn't possibly let things progress naturally and make love in front of the fire—Tim might walk in at any second. Which left going to her bedroom and the embarrassment of silently getting undressed, of having to keep their voices—and moans—low, just in case they woke Tim.

She tore herself away.

What was she *thinking* of? She didn't want to make love to him!

He had never been so frustrated in his life. 'Lisi—'

'No!' She shook her head vehemently. 'I am *not* going to have sex with you, Philip. The first time was bad enough—'

'I beg to differ,' he murmured, thinking how magnificent she looked when she was angry.

She carried on as if he hadn't interrupted. 'When I discovered you were married I felt like hell—but at least I thought that you had been so overcome with desire that you had been unable to stop yourself. Desire for *me*,' she finished deliberately.

His eyes narrowed as he tried to work out exactly what she was getting at. 'I'm not sure that I understand you, Lisi.'

'It didn't even have to be me, did it? I was just a vessel for your more basic needs!' she carried on wildly. 'Anyone would have done! Your wife was sick and you were frustrated—that's what really happened, isn't it, Philip?'

He went rigid. 'My God,' he said, in disgust. 'You really know how to twist the knife, don't you?' He picked up his overcoat and walked to the front door and opened it without another word.

She wanted to call after him, to take back the hateful words which had seemed to come pouring out of her mouth like poison, but one look at the icy expression on his face as he turned round made her realise that it would be a futile gesture.

He gave a cold, hard smile. 'If your idea was to insult me so much that I would go away and never come back again, then you have just very nearly succeeded,' he said.

And, bizarrely, the thought that her hurt pride and resentment might have cost Tim a relationship with his father wounded her far more than anything else. 'Philip—'

He shook his head. 'Please don't say any more—I don't think I could take it. I'd better just tell you that this particular campaign won't work. You see, Tim is far more important to me than the obvious loathing you feel for me. I'm here, Lisi—and I'm here for the duration. Better get used to it.'

And without another word, he was gone.

CHAPTER NINE

MARIAN Reece pursed her lips together in a silent whistle. 'Good heavens—just how much do you think he's spending on that property?'

Lisi looked up from her computer, and, lo and behold—another upmarket van was cruising past the office towards The Old Rectory. What was it this time? Lisi peered out of the window and read from the gold lettering on the side of the van. 'Tricia Brady; Superior Interiors'. 'He's obviously having the place decorated now,' she said, with a sigh.

Marian's eyes goggled. 'And how!' she exclaimed. 'I've heard of her—she must have come all the way down from London. This early in the New Year, too—I'm surprised she wasn't fully booked.'

'She probably was,' said Lisi gloomily. 'She's probably got long blonde hair and legs up to her armpits and Philip probably just outrageously batted those beautiful eyes at her and she probably cancelled every engagement in her diary!'

Marian gave her a shrewd look. 'Do I detect a sign of the green-eyed monster?' she asked.

Lisi replaced the gloomy look with a fairly good impression of devil-may-care. 'Not at all,' she said airily. 'I expect that's exactly what happened. Either that or he's paying well over the odds.'

'He must be,' said Marian. 'It's only the middle of January—and already he's transformed the place! I've never known builders be quite so willing, or so efficient!'

'No,' said Lisi tonelessly.

Marian shot her a glance. 'How's it going between you two?'

'It's not between *us* two,' replied Lisi carefully. 'The only relationship I have with Philip is that we happen to share a child.'

'Only?' spluttered Marian, then sighed. 'And is it...amicable?'

Lisi sighed. She had vowed to keep it that way, but ever since her outburst on Christmas night he had been keeping his distance from her. He had been round three times to see Tim, and the atmosphere had been awkward, to say the least.

For a start, the house always seemed so much smaller when he was in it, and the unspoken tension between them was so strong that Lisi was surprised that Tim wasn't made uncomfortable by it.

But no. Tim didn't seem to notice anything or anyone—he was so enraptured by the man he had almost immediately taken to calling 'Daddy'.

The first time he'd done it, Lisi had spoken to him gently at bedtime that night. 'You don't have to say Daddy if you don't want to,' she suggested gently. 'Philip won't mind being called just Philip, I'm sure.'

He didn't answer and she wasn't even sure if he had registered her words or not, but he obviously had, because at the end of Saturday's visit Philip paused on his way out of the front door, his eyes spitting with undisguised rage.

'Did you tell Tim not to call me Daddy?' he demanded.

She sighed. 'That's not what I said at all.'

'That's what he told me!'

She kept her voice low, tried to stay calm, though heaven only knew—it wasn't easy. 'I merely suggested that he might find it easier to call you Philip. For the time being—'

'Until *you* decided that the time was right, I suppose?'

he questioned witheringly. 'And when would that be, Lisi? Some time? Never?'

She stuck to her guns. She was not going to let his hostility get to her. *She was not.* 'I just didn't want him to feel that he was being railroaded into anything—'

'By me?'

'Not by anyone!' she retorted, her voice rising. 'It's just such a huge thing to suddenly start calling you Daddy!'

He had moved a little closer, his body language just short of menacing—so how come she didn't feel in the least bit intimidated by it? How come she wanted to tell him to forget their stupid rows and to kiss her like he had done on Christmas night?

'Or is it just that *you* feel threatened by it, Lisi?'

'Threatened? Me?'

'Yes, you! Unwilling to share him, are you? Do you want all his love for yourself, is that it?'

'Oh, don't talk such rubbish!' she snapped. 'I was thinking of *Tim*!'

'So you claim. When it would clearly suit you far more to have me as far away from you as possible! Well, just don't use him as a pawn in our little disagreement—do you understand, Lisi!'

Little disagreement? If this was his idea of a little disagreement, then she'd hate to enter into all-out warfare with him!

Marian was still staring at her with a question in her eyes, and Lisi shook her head.

'No,' she said slowly, in answer to her boss's question. 'It isn't exactly what I'd call amicable—even though that's what we both wanted originally.'

'You should talk to him about it!' urged Marian.

But there didn't seem anything left to say, thought Lisi as she picked up the telephone which had just begun to ring. 'Good afternoon, Homefinders Agency.'

'Lisi? It's Philip.'

Of course it was Philip—no one else had a voice that rich, that deep, that dark. 'Hello, Philip,' she said, cursing her body's reaction as she felt the inevitable prickle of excitement. 'What can I do for you?'

Silently, he cursed. How shocked she would be if he answered that question truthfully.

'I'm up at the house,' he said.

'Here?' she questioned stupidly, her heart racing. 'In the village?'

'Yeah. I drove up early this morning.'

He was here, just down the road and he hadn't even bothered to tell her he was coming. Just why that should hurt so much she didn't know, but it did.

'I'm having the house decorated,' he was saying. 'Someone is over here now with some sample fabrics.'

She certainly wasn't going to pander to his ego by telling him that she had seen the plush van driving by. 'Really?' she asked pleasantly.

'Really,' he echoed, mocking her insincere tone. 'And I wondered whether you were free for half an hour?'

Her pulse began to race. 'Why?'

She could be so damned abrupt, he thought. 'I didn't know if you wanted to choose some colours for Tim's room.'

Time stopped. He seemed to be speaking in some strange, terrible language. 'T-Tim's room?' she croaked.

Something in the way she said it made him want to offer reassurance, until he remembered her monstrous accusation on Christmas night, and he hardened his heart against the tremor in her voice. Did she think that *he* didn't have feelings, too?

'That's right. He will *need* his own room, Lisi—surely you realise that?'

The only thing she realised was that she was fighting to

control her breath. 'I have to discuss this with you, and we can't do it on the phone,' she said.

'Then come up to the house.'

'I'm working.'

'Doesn't Marian owe you a few hours? For your unscheduled work when I demanded that you show me around the rectory?'

'I'll ask her,' she said, in a low voice. 'I can't promise anything.'

His voice sounded noncommittal. 'Suit yourself. It's up to you, Lisi—you're the one who wants to talk.'

She put the phone down, feeling close to tears, and saw Marian looking at her with concern.

'Philip?' she asked.

'How did you guess?'

'Normal clients don't usually leave the agent looking as though the bottom has just fallen out of their world.'

Maybe it just had. Lisi cleared her throat. 'Marian— would it be possible to take an hour off? I need to talk to Philip and he's up at the rectory.'

'Of course it would.' Marian hesitated. 'Listen, my dear—have you thought about consulting a lawyer?'

Lisi shook her head. 'There's no point—it would achieve precisely nothing. He isn't being unreasonable. Tim adores him. He's his father—by law he is *allowed* contact. It's just me who has the problem with it.'

Marian nodded. 'Take as long as you need.'

Lisi gathered up her coat and wrapped herself up in it, but once outside it seemed to offer little protection against the bitter wind, although maybe it was the bitter heartache which was making her teeth chatter.

She trudged up the lane to The Old Rectory, and for a moment she stood stock-still with amazement, for she had seen the comings and goings of various vans and contractors, but had deliberately stayed away from the place, telling herself that it would be too traumatic to see her former home being completely changed.

But her amazement was tinged with admiration, because, whatever Philip was doing inside the house, on the outside, at least—his taste could not be faulted.

The exterior had been painted a cool, pale grey and all the mildew had been removed. Window frames were gleaming, as was the newly painted front door, and the garden had obviously been lovingly attacked by experts.

The front door was slightly ajar, and when she received no reply to her knock she pushed it open and walked into the hall where another shock awaited her. The walls were a deep, vibrant scarlet—red as holly berries—and the floorboards gleaming, with an exquisite long, silk runner in shades of deepest cobalt and scarlet and jade.

It looked utterly beautiful, she thought, and a lump rose in her throat as she called.

'Hello?'

'Hello, Lisi,' came a voice from upstairs. 'Come on up—we're up here.'

We? And then she remembered the interior design van.

With reluctant feet she made her way slowly upstairs in the direction of the voices she could hear speaking and laughing, and she felt a wave of objection that he should feel happy enough to laugh while her world seemed to be caving in.

To her horror, the voices were coming from the direction of a room she knew only too well—her old childhood bedroom—and her heart sank even further. Had he known, or guessed, she wondered, or was it simply coincidence which had made Philip select that particular room for Tim?

Drawing a deep breath, she walked straight in, and then stopped.

Two heads were bent close over a swatch of fabrics—one dark and nut-brown, the other blonde, and Lisi almost gave a hollow laugh. She had imagined Tricia Brady to be blonde with legs up to her armpits, and in that she had been uncannily accurate—but she had imagined the blonde hair to have come out of a bottle and for an aging face to be caked in heavy make-up.

But this woman fulfilled none of those criteria.

Her shiny blonde hair was fair and pale and completely natural, and when she lifted her head at the sound of Lisi's footsteps she didn't appear to be wearing any make-up at all. But then she didn't need to—skin that flawless and china-blue eyes that saucer-like did not need any help from nature to enhance them.

She was dressed practically and yet stunningly—in a pair of butter-soft suede trousers which must have cost what Lisi earned in a month. A cream silk shirt and a sheepskin-lined waistcoat completed the look and Lisi shuddered to think what her off-the-peg department store workaday suit must look like in comparison.

Philip smiled, but the expression on his face was as cool as it had been since Christmas. 'Lisi, hi,' he said. 'This is Tricia Brady—she's helping me with decor for the house.'

She's helping me. It didn't sound like a strictly working relationship, did it? thought Lisi indignantly. He could have said, Tricia is the designer, or, Tricia is working for me.

'Hello,' she said, thinking how wooden her voice sounded. 'I'm pleased to meet you.'

'Me, too.' Tricia grinned. 'I would shake hands, but my fingers are freezing—I keep telling Philip to turn the heating up, but he won't listen!'

'That's because people tend to go to sleep if it's too warm. Not good—but especially not good for people who are working,' he responded drily, but flashed her an answering smile.

Lisi felt sick, but she guessed that this was something she was going to have to get used to. If it wasn't Tricia it would be someone else. Some beautiful, expensively dressed woman who would temporarily or permanently share Philip's life one day.

And become a surrogate mother to Tim while he was here, she reminded herself, gritting her teeth behind a smile which pride forced her to make.

'Lisi is the mother of my son,' explained Philip. 'And so I thought she could give us some input on colours and fabrics.'

It was the coldest and most distancing description he could have given her—and yet, when she thought about it, how else could he have put it? She wasn't his girlfriend—current *or past*.

Pulling herself together, she walked over and looked down at the swatch of fabrics which Tricia was still holding. 'May I?' she asked pleasantly, and Tricia handed it to her.

She pretended to lose herself in them, though her mind was only half on the task—but she had spotted immediately the one which Tim would like the most.

'This one,' and she jabbed at the brightly coloured piece of material which depicted Mickey Mouse dancing all over it.

'Lisi likes Disney,' Philip explained with a smile, thinking how jerky and unnatural her movements were. 'She always has done, haven't you, Lisi?'

He was remembering her birthday cake, and so was she. That innocent start to a supposed friendship which had brought so much heartache in its wake. She nodded. 'Wh-what colour are you planning to do the walls?'

Tricia peered down at the fabric and pointed a perfect fingernail at several of the colours. 'We could pick out one of these shades,' she suggested and turned her head. 'What do you think, Phil?'

Phil?

Phil?

Lisi wanted to scream and to demand what right she had to call him by a nickname that *she* had never heard used before, but there was absolutely no point at all. Tricia could call him anything she liked, and probably did—in bed at night when he was making mad, passionate love to her.

'I like the...I like the yellow.' She swallowed.

'Mmm!' Tricia smiled. 'Perfect! Sunny and positive—and with all that glorious light flooding in—' She waved an expansive arm at the window. 'The room will look irresistible!' She shot a look at Philip, and her eyes glimmered. 'We could do it in the same colour as your London dining room, in fact—or would you rather something different down here?'

'Something a touch brighter, perhaps?' he murmured as Lisi turned abruptly away.

So Tricia had decorated his other home, too, had she? That was a pretty big compliment to pay a woman, no matter that she was being paid for her skills. To be selected to choose paints and fabrics for a man as discerning as Philip must mean that he rated her very highly indeed.

Lisi walked over to the window and looked out, the way she had done countless times before, as a child. She used to sit on the ledge for hours and watch the change as each new season came upon the garden, though she could never remember a scene so bare and unforgiving as the one which lay outside today.

'Shall we tackle the main bedroom today?' Tricia was asking.

Philip was watching Lisi and saw the way that her body had stiffened and some pernicious devil made him want to take Tricia up on her offer, but he decided against it.

'Not today, thanks, Trish,' he said casually. 'I have a few things I need to discuss with Lisi.'

'Oh. Okay. Well, call me later, if you like, and we'll sort out what needs doing. Nice to have met you, Lisi!'

Lisi turned around, wishing that her features would stop feeling as if they were made out of stone. 'Nice to have met you, too,' she managed.

There was silence in the room while Tricia gathered up her samples and put them all in a soft leather case, then she stood on tiptoe and kissed first Philip's right cheek, and then his left.

'See ya!' She smiled. 'I'll let myself out.'

'I'll call you,' he promised.

Lisi studied the floorboards with intense interest and not a word was spoken as they heard Tricia running down the stairs and the front door slamming behind her.

'Lisi?' he questioned softly.

She lifted her eyes to find herself imprisoned in a cool green gaze and her cheeks flooded with heat as she gave into the unwelcome but inevitable.

I want him, she thought suddenly, and the tip of her tongue flicked out to lick at the sudden unbearable dryness of her lips. I always have and I always will—and I can't bear the thought of anyone else having him. If he still wants me—*if*—then who on earth am I benefitting by turning him down? He is tied to me through Tim, she told herself with a fierce, primitive feeling of possession—and he will always be tied to me.

Now what was she playing at? he wondered. Why was she giving him that flushed and glittering look as though she wanted him to go and take her in his arms—especially as she had made so clear on Christmas night that physical closeness was the very last thing on her mind. Damn her! he thought, feeling his body immediately reacting to what looked like an unmistakable invitation in her eyes.

She didn't break the stare, just carried on looking at him, feeling her body begin to flower with need as his eyes darkened and then narrowed in a slowly dawning comprehension.

'Lisi?' he said again, only now his voice had thickened to honey. 'What the hell do you think you're doing?'

She wasn't going to play games; there was no time for games, and even if there were—wouldn't games be totally inappropriate between a couple who had been through what they had been through?

She moistened her lips again and saw the dull flush of awareness arrow up the carved cheekbones. 'Is Tricia *just* your designer?' she asked.

Her question told him everything. She was jealous. *Jealous!* He felt the heady flood of triumph as he realised that now he had her exactly where he wanted her.

'And if she is?'

The instant denial she had been preying for had not materialised, but his ambiguous question did nothing but fuel the fire which was slowly building inside her.

'Yes, or no?'

'What's it to you, Lisi? Don't you like me having women friends?'

'No!' The word shot out all by itself before she could stop it.

He could see the tension building in her—he would build it and build it until it all came rushing out and she would be unable to stop it. His question was silky. 'Why not?'

Damn him! Was he going to make her beg? She wanted him, yes, but she would never, ever beg. Her breathing was so shallow and erratic that she could barely get the words out. 'You know why not.'

Oh, yes, he knew. He could tell just by looking at her. She shouldn't be able to appear so damned sexy—not in that dull, chain-store suit with her hair scraped right back off her face. Some men might have been turned on by Tricia's blonde, pampered perfection—but he wanted this complex, beguiling woman who could not disguise the hunger in her eyes.

'Come here,' he ordered softly.

Pride forgotten, she went to him, staring up at him with wide eyes, praying for him to take the next step and to pull her into his arms. But he did not touch her. Not straight away. His eyes were mocking her and enchanting her, his lips curved into a predatory smile.

'What do you want, Lisi? Tell me.'

Peace of mind, that was what she wanted—and she suspected that she would never get it with Philip Caprice in her life, in whatever capacity. She tipped her head to one side and wondered whether she could break *him*.

'Don't you know?' she responded shakily.

Something snapped inside him as he realised that he had wasted enough time. Tease her too much and she might just turn on her high heels and walk right out of here and he might never get another opportunity to discover whether she was as dynamic as he remembered, or whether time had distorted the memory and made it into something it wasn't.

He reached to her hair and removed the restraining clip and her hair tumbled free. 'Beautiful,' he murmured unsteadily as he pulled her into his arms and bent his head and she could feel his hot breath on her face.

'Are you jealous, Lisi?' he taunted. 'Jealous of Tricia?'

Jealous of every woman who might end up in his arms, like this. 'Yes,' she whispered.

His laugh was a low sound of victory as he bent his mouth to hers, teasing it open with the elusive flicker of his tongue, and Lisi closed her eyes and gave into it, snaking her hands up to the broad shoulders as he levered her up close to him.

He could feel her breasts pushing against him—their fullness growing by the second—and something primal exploded inside him in a ferment of desire so blisteringly hot that he shuddered in its power, scarcely aware of his actions as he began to feverishly unbutton her suit jacket.

She knew exactly what he was doing, and that she ought to stop him, that they shouldn't be doing this now, here, but the moment his hand cupped at her breast Lisi knew she was lost.

'Philip,' she cried.

Through the mists of wanting, her broken little cry penetrated. 'What?'

She shook her head. 'Philip, Philip, Philip,' she said, over and over again, and his name tasted as delicious as the warm lips which were plundering hers so expertly, so that she felt as if she were drowning in sheer forbidden pleasure.

He pushed the jacket from her shoulders and it fell to the floor, and then he unbuttoned her white blouse and sucked in a shivering breath as he looked down at her breasts. Rich, ripe breasts, covered by some washed-out looking bra which had clearly seen better days. But none of that mattered, not when each tight little bud was so clearly defined.

With a small moan he reached his hand round her back and unclipped the bra in a fluid gesture until it dropped redundantly to join the jacket, and her breasts were free.

She jerked her head back with a moan as she felt the first hot lick of his tongue teasing each nipple into near-painful awareness. He was unbuttoning her skirt now and sliding the zip down and she wanted him to, couldn't wait for him to touch her where she so squirmingly needed to be touched. The room was cool, but all she could feel was the heat of his hands and his mouth as they trailed paths of delight over the skin he was swiftly uncovering.

She was down to her panties and tights now, and Philip pulled impatiently at his belt, silently groaning at the necessary delay of getting free from this damned clothing. Her fingers were scrabbling at his sweater and he momentarily moved away from her so that he could haul it over his head, and pulled her back again so that her breasts nudged so enchantingly against his bare chest.

She was clumsily jerking at the zip now and he shook his head, stilling her hand and moving it away while he dealt with it, because he was so aroused that it needed a man's hand to protect his straining hardness.

Shoes and socks and boxers were kicked and pulled off and he unceremoniously hoicked her tights and panties off before tossing them disdainfully into the corner. 'I'm going to buy you stockings,' he promised unsteadily. 'From now on you will wear nothing but stockings!'

She neither knew nor cared what he was intending to do, apart from what lay in the immediate future.

'Are you still on the pill?' he was demanding.

She shook her head. 'Not any more.'

He grabbed his trousers and pulled a pack of condoms out, thanking some merciful hand which had guided him to buy some. 'I'd like you to slide this on for me, Lisi,' he whispered as he ripped open the foil. 'Come on. Put it on for me.'

She glanced down, and swallowed. She couldn't, not this first time—it was too daunting, too intimate. 'You do it,' she whispered back.

She felt him sliding the condom on, then heard him swear softly, and when she opened her eyes to see what was the matter he was glowering down at the bare floorboards with a look of disgust on his face.

'There's no bloody bed in the house yet!' he groaned, and swiftly picked her up to carry her to the other side of the room, out of view of the window.

'Wh-what are you doing?' She gasped as he leaned her

back against the wall and lifted her up, positioning her legs around his naked waist.

'What do you think I'm doing?' he ground out. His fingers moved down to find her slick and ready and he uttered silent thanks because he felt as if he would go insane unless he…he…

'Oh, Philip,' she sobbed as his great strength thrust into her, and she thought that nothing could ever feel this good, or this right. 'Philip,' she said again, on a long-drawn-out shudder.

Her pleasure only intensified his. He had never had to fight to maintain control quite so much as he moved inside her, watching her face as it bloomed, feeling her hot tightness encasing him in a moist, exquisite sheath.

He sought to distract himself with words rather than sensation. 'Tell me how it feels,' he urged throatily.

How to describe paradise in a sentence? she despaired with another helpless moan as he cupped her buttocks and thrust into her even deeper.

'Tell me!' he commanded.

'It's…it's…'

'It's what, Lisi?' he prompted, his voice a silken caress.

It's Philip, the father of my child, she thought as the unbelievable waves of orgasm crept unexpectedly upon her, sweeping her up in their swell, rocking her until she was left shuddering and weak, her tears spilling down like rain onto his shoulder.

Her tears confused him, acted as a temporary deterrent to his own fulfilment. For a second he almost wanted to lift her head and dry her tears away, demand that she tell him what had made her cry like that, but his own orgasm was too strong to be denied. Even as he began to frame the question he felt himself caught in its inexorable path, and he drove into her, pulled her closer still until his seed spilled out, and he was rocked with the force of it all.

Seconds—minutes?—later, he kissed the top of her head and felt her shiver.

'You're cold,' he observed. 'Better get dressed.'

So that was it. Wild and passionate sex up against the wall and all he could talk about was the temperature of the room.

Reminding herself that she had wanted it as much—if not more—than him, Lisi nodded and snuggled against his chest for one last precious moment of physical closeness, listening to the muffled thunder of his heart as it began to slow.

He could have stayed like this all day. Still inside her, with her naked body locked so indulgently around his and her hair spilling all over him—making everything black where it touched. He felt himself begin to stir again and knew that, if one of them did not begin to make an effort to get dressed, he would grow inside her to fill her again, and want to make love with the same sweet abandon as before.

'You acted like you really needed that,' he observed in a whisper.

She lifted her eyes to his and suddenly thought—tell him. Why not? 'It's…it's been a long time,' she admitted.

'How long?' he demanded, though his body tensed as it prepared itself for the stab of jealousy.

'Since that night with you,' she answered slowly and heard him suck in a disbelieving breath.

His eyes narrowed. 'Honestly?'

'There's no reason for me to lie, Philip.'

'I'm flattered,' he murmured.

Ridiculously disappointed by his reaction, she let her feet slide slowly to the ground. 'I have to get back to work,' she said.

He thought how matter-of-fact she sounded—still, if that was the way she wanted to play it, it was fine by him. At least there were to be no hypocritical words of love and affection, which neither of them would mean. 'There's hot water,' he offered. 'If you want to take a shower?'

Lisi blushed. She hadn't thought that she would have to go back all sticky and redolent of the scent of their sex—but she wouldn't, not really. Unlike last time, he had used a condom.

'Use the bathroom off the main bedroom,' he suggested. 'It's—'

'I know where it is, thank you, Philip,' she said impatiently, shaking her head. 'I used to live here, remember?' And then *she* remembered just which room they were in.

He felt her tense. 'What's the matter?'

She bit her lip as she reached for her underwear. 'This used to be *my* room,' she moaned. 'And soon it will be Tim's, and we've just…just…'

'Just had sex in it?'

Lisi turned away before he could see her face. He could not have termed it in a more insulting way. 'Yes,' she said tonelessly, and suddenly the desire and the passion which had made her want him so very badly—seemed like the worst idea she had ever had in her life.

'Lisi?'

Despairing at the hope which leapt up inside her, she turned around again. 'What?'

'Here!' He threw over her blouse and noted that she caught it like an athlete. 'There's nothing wrong with what we just did,' he said softly. 'It's as natural and as old as time. So what if it *is* going to be Tim's room—how can what we just did in here possibly harm him? It's how he got here in the first place, after all!'

'I don't need you to give me a basic lesson in sex education,' she said crossly, pulling her skirt up over her hips and zipping it up.

No, she certainly didn't. He had never met a woman so

free and generous in her love-making before. Still slightly reeling from learning that there had been no other lover, he came over and began to button up her blouse for her, tempted to lay the flat of his hands over the magnificent thrust of her breasts, but her unsmiling face told him not to bother trying.

'What's the matter?' he asked quietly. 'Are you regretting what just happened?'

There was no reason to be anything other than truthful—not now. Too much water had passed underneath the bridge for coyness or prevarication.

'A little. Aren't you?'

He shrugged as he slipped his shoes on. 'There's no point in feeling regret—you know it was inevitable.'

'I don't understand.'

'I think you do.' His eyes pierced her with their green light. 'Don't you think we *needed* that? To get rid of some of the tension between us?'

'You make it sound so…so…'

'So what, Lisi?'

'So *functional*.' She shuddered.

'Sometimes sex is. We were always going to have trouble creating the candlelight and roses scene, weren't we—what with Tim being around and your obvious low opinion of me?' He picked up his jacket. 'So what happened to make you change your mind about hating me? Was it purely jealousy—because you thought that I had something going with Tricia?'

'And do you?' she asked boldly, 'You never did answer that.'

The question angered him. 'You really think I would have just had sex with you, if I was involved with Tricia?'

She wanted to say that he had done once before, except that now she was beginning to look at that night differently. Could a man who was married to a woman who lay in a deep coma be considered married in the true sense of the word? She looked at him and shook her head, some bone-deep certainty giving her an answer she had not expected. 'No,' she said quietly. 'I don't.'

He expelled a long, pent-up sigh. 'Well, thanks for that, at least.'

'I have to go.' She straightened her jacket and at that moment felt almost close to him, though maybe that was just nature's way of justifying what they had just been doing. But she plucked up the courage to ask another question, one which had been praying on her mind for much longer. 'Philip?'

He narrowed his eyes. 'What?'

'What made you make love to me?' She saw the gleam in his eyes and hastily shook her head. 'No, not this time— last time. When you didn't really…know me…nor I you. Was it just lust? Me being in the wrong place at the wrong time?'

For a long time he had thought that it was simply lust— but if that were the case, then why hadn't he followed up one of the countless other invitations which had come his way? He remembered what Khalim had said, but then Khalim was a born romantic. He shook his head, knowing that he owed her his honesty. 'That's just it, Lisi—I don't know.'

It was not the answer she had wanted—but it was better than nothing.

'Listen,' he said, and she prayed for some sweetener, something to tell her that she wasn't just Lisi-the-body, but Lisi a woman who was entitled to a modicum of respect.

'What?'

'Can I come to the nursery with you later, when you collect Tim?'

It would be his first 'outing' as Tim's father and she knew that she could not refuse him—but he hadn't needed to make love to her first to ensure that she said yes. She nodded. The only way forward was with truth and honesty and no game-playing. She wasn't going to regret what she had been unable to resist, and neither was she going to use Tim as a pawn to try to make her feel better about her mixed-up emotions.

She smiled. 'Of course you can,' she said simply, but the smile cost her almost as much as the words to make.

CHAPTER TEN

MARIAN glanced across the office. 'Telephone, Lisi.' She smiled. 'For you. It's Philip.'

Lisi reached out for the phone. As if she needed to be told! Marian's gooey expression said it all, because her boss seemed to be labouring under the illusion that all was hunky-dory between the two of them.

She sighed. Maybe that was what it looked like to the outside world. He visited Langley nearly every weekend and he took the three of them to the zoo and to parks. Dragged them on long walks around the beautiful countryside. Tim liked it that way and so, stupidly, did she.

Philip had even started teaching Tim to play football and she had watched the bond between them grow and grow, happy for her son that it should be so, convincing herself that it did not mean that she was in any way marginalised.

But he had made no further attempt to make love to her again, and, while she didn't know why, she couldn't bring herself to ask him. She feared that once had been enough for him. He had got all the hunger out of his system and now he could move on. What choice did she have, other than to respect and accept that, even though in the long, restless nights her body ached for him?

She still wanted him like crazy, and she guessed that she always would—certainly no man had ever captured her quite so completely, neither before nor since. But sex complicated things and sex with Philip sent her whole world spinning into a vortex of confusion.

Sex with Philip made you long for the impossible—the

impossible in this case being his love. And in her heart she knew she would never have that.

'Hello?'

'Hi. How are things?'

'Good.' He only ever rang her at the office, and part of her wondered whether this was because this guaranteed her polite courtesy towards him. Perhaps he thought that she would not be nearly so compliant if she didn't have Marian half listening in on the conversation. And if he thought that, then he was a fool—because all the fight and hostility had left her. Sex could complicate things, yes—but it could also help define what was most important, and Lisi knew, rightly or wrongly, that she loved him with a fervour which made her ache for him.

'How's life in the big metropolis?' she asked.

'How long have you got?' he asked, with a short laugh, thinking that the quiet village life of Langley was the one true oasis in his high-powered life these days. 'It's busy, crowded, pressured, competitive. Want more?'

Lots more. More than he would ever give her. She laughed back. 'I think I get the picture.' She waited. Was today's request going to be the one she most dreaded? That he would ask if Tim could spend the night at The Old Rectory with him alone, and the separation of their lives as joint parents would begin? She had been astonished that he hadn't asked already, when the bright yellow room with its Mickey Mouse curtains had been ready for occupation since mid-January, and they were now well into April.

'I was wondering whether you were free on Saturday?' he asked.

'Saturday? Of course I am—why?'

He thought that most women might have pretended to think about it. 'There's a ball I have to attend up here— it's usually pretty good fun. I know it's short notice, but I wondered whether you'd like to come?'

'As your guest?' she asked stupidly.

'I wasn't planning on asking you to be my chauffeur!' Had he been instrumental in heightening her insecurity? His voice softened. 'Of course as my guest!'

'I don't know whether I can get a babysitter for Tim, not this late. And anyway, I don't know if I'd want to leave him while I went up to London,' she added doubtfully.

'You wouldn't have to. I want you to bring him—an old friend of mine has offered to babysit. It's all arranged, if you're agreed?'

Her heart was pounding with excitement. Oh, for goodness' sake—calm down, Lisi! she told herself. Somebody else has probably let him down at the last minute.

'Well?'

She swallowed. 'Okay,' she replied, as casually as she could. 'I'd love to.'

'Good.' There was a pause. 'And I'd like to buy you something to wear.'

Lisi froze, and her fingers tightened around the receiver. 'I'm not sure that I understand what you mean,' she said icily.

'Something nice—a pretty dress. Whatever you like,' he amended hastily.

So he was ashamed of his country bumpkin, was he? 'What's the matter, Philip?' she asked sarcastically. 'Afraid that I'll turn up in something completely inappropriate and let you down?'

He sighed. Hadn't he anticipated just this response? She could be so damned *proud* about some things. Like her dogged insistence on paying her share whenever the three of them went out. Time after time she had infuriated him by letting him pay for Tim, but not her, and he worried about how much their outings were eating into her limited budget.

'That wasn't what I meant!' he protested.

'Well, that's what it sounded like!'

'Let's call it a Christmas present, then,' he said placatingly. 'Since I didn't buy you one.'

They had scarcely been able to be civil to one another at the time, so that was hardly surprising, but Lisi felt the slow pulse of anger ticking away inside her. Anything more designed to make her feel like a kept woman, she could not imagine!

'Thanks, but no thanks,' she said shortly. 'I'm sure that I can dig *something* suitable out!'

Philip sighed, recognising a stubbornness which would not be shifted, no matter how he played it. 'Okay, Lisi. Have it your own way. I'll arrange to have a car pick you and Tim up on Saturday afternoon—let's say about three. Does that suit you?'

'I can get the train!'

'Yes, you can—but you aren't going to,' he argued grimly. 'It'll take you for ever, and I'm sure that Tim would enjoy travelling in a big, shiny car.'

Yes, he would absolutely love it—of course he would. Philip could give Tim all kinds of expensive toys which she would never be able to. Perhaps that was why he always rang her at work—so that she would not be able to point out little home truths like that one.

'Shall we say three?' he persisted.

'Yes, Philip. We'll be ready. Goodbye,' and she put the phone down to find Marian watching her.

'What's happened?' she asked quickly.

'He's invited the two of us up to London. He's sending a car, he's arranged a babysitter for Tim and he's taking me to a ball.'

'Oh, for heaven's sake, Lisi!' exclaimed Marian. 'I thought he'd given you bad news! Why on earth are you sitting there with such a long face? What woman wouldn't give the earth for an invitation like that?'

Lisi forced a smile. If only it were as simple as Marian seemed to think it was. 'I'm sure it will be very enjoyable,' she agreed evenly and saw Marian shake her head in disbelief.

She told an excited Tim, and that night, after she had tucked him up in bed and read him his story, she went into her bedroom to survey the contents of her wardrobe.

Ballgowns were long and she had precisely two long dresses—one she had worn during her pregnancy and which now looked like a tent, while the other was flower-sprigged and hopelessly outdated. She zipped it up. And cheap.

Had she been out of her mind to refuse Philip his offer of a dress?

She pulled a grim face at the milk-maid image reflected back at her from the mirror.

No. She would not be in any way beholden to him. By hook or by crook she would make a transformation as total as Cinderella's had been.

She just wasn't sure how!

The next morning she left Tim with Rachel and Blaine while she went to the nearby town of Bilchester to investigate its ballgown possibilities, but after two hours spent solidly trudging from shop to shop she was approaching a state close to despair.

The kind of dress which an evening with Philip would require would create an impossibly huge hole in her tight budget.

'Why don't you hire?' suggested an assistant at her very last port of call.

Lisi shrugged, her naturally parsimonious streak baulking at paying out good money for a dress she would only get to wear once. 'I want something to show for my money,' she admitted.

The assistant grinned. 'Makes a nice change to get someone in here who isn't completely rolling in it!' She lowered her voice as the manageress drifted past in a heavy cloud of cloying perfume. 'Have you tried the thrift shops?' she questioned.

'Thrift shops?'

'Charity shops,' the assistant amended. 'There are two here in Bilchester, and it's such a rich area that you never know what you'll pick up. I shop there myself,' she confided. 'I get staff discount in here, but the stuff is way too expensive.'

'What a brilliant idea!' said Lisi, with a grateful smile. 'Thanks!'

In the second charity shop she could scarcely believe her luck, because she looked in the window and found her dream dress staring her right in the face.

It looked old—but fashionably old—as if someone had bought this dress many years ago and looked after it with loving care. It had a tight, strapless silk bodice from which the many-layered tulle skirt flared out like a black cloud. It was a fairy-tale dress.

An elderly woman behind the till saw her looking at it.

'Beautiful, isn't it?' She smiled.

'Exquisite.'

'Only came in this morning—must have cost someone a fortune.'

'Can I...can I try it on, please?' asked Lisi breathlessly.

The woman wrinkled her nose. 'We're not really supposed to take it out of the window for a month.'

'Oh, please,' begged Lisi. '*Please.*' And the next moment she found herself telling the woman all about Philip—well, not *all*, but the bit about going to the fancy ball and refusing his offer of a dress.

'How can I refuse after a story like that? I'll get it out of the window. But don't get your hopes up too much—it might not fit. The waist is absolutely tiny.'

But it did. Just. Lisi breathed in and knew a moment's anxiety as the assistant struggled slightly with the zip, but once up, it fitted as though it had been designed for her.

'I won't be able to eat a thing!' she groaned.

'You won't want to, I shouldn't think. Looking like that I doubt whether you'll leave the dance-floor all night!'

It was the most beautiful thing she had ever worn. Tiny sequins were dotted here and there over the skirt, so that they glittered and caught the light as she moved. 'I'll take it,' she said instantly. 'Provided that I can afford it!'

'I'll make sure you can!' The woman gave a dreamy smile. 'It's such a romantic story!'

If only she knew! Still, she was not going to dwell on what she hadn't got—she was going to enjoy what she had—and a ball with Philip sounded pretty near perfect.

The car arrived on Saturday at three o'clock on the dot—an outrageously luxurious vehicle, complete with a uniformed chauffeur, and Tim squealed in excitement, and chatted incessantly for the whole journey.

'Calm down, poppet,' murmured Lisi, thinking that if he carried on at this rate they would never get him settled for the night.

But when the car drew up outside a house situated in a quiet, leafy lane in Hampstead, Lisi very nearly asked the chauffeur to take them straight back home again.

She swallowed. She had known that Philip was rich, of course she had—but not *this* rich, because the house she glimpsed as the car purred its way up the drive was more the size of a small castle! And land in London was unbelievably expensive—so just how wealthy *was* he to be able to afford a plot this size?

'*Big* house, Mummy!' squealed Tim excitedly.

Why hadn't he told her? Prepared her? She twisted the strap of her handbag nervously. But what could he have said that wouldn't have sounded like boasting? And Philip was not a boastful man, she realised. He carried his obvious success with an air of cool understatement.

Nevertheless, her heart was still beating like a piston when he opened the door before she had a chance to knock and the sight of him on his home territory quite took her breath away, and drove all thoughts of his intimidating wealth away.

He was wearing black jeans and a soft blue cashmere sweater and his dark hair was ruffled and his eyes very green, if a little wary.

'I wasn't sure if you'd pull out at the last minute,' he admitted.

'At least I'm not wholly predictable!'

Predictable? Never, ever. He still hadn't got over that highly erotic scene in her old bedroom. He felt his heart accelerate and he silently cursed himself for breaking his self-imposed promise not to dwell on that. For once, with Lisi—he was going to make his head dictate events, and not his body.

'Hello, Tim,' he said softly and crouched down to smile on a level with the boy. 'Come on in.'

Tim was strangely silent, but he slid his little hand into Philip's proffered one and went inside.

Lisi was too excited and nervous to take much in except for the feeling of light and space and exquisite decor.

'Shall we have tea in the sitting room first?' Philip asked. 'You can have the guided tour later.'

Tea was all laid out on a table by a roaring log fire—a proper, old-fashioned tea with sandwiches and scones and cake and biscuits. Tim gave a little whimper of delight, which turned into a whoop when he spotted the wooden train-set which had been laid out beneath the window, and he dashed over to it immediately. It was just like the one he had at home, Lisi noted. Only bigger.

Wondering just how she would be able to bring him—

and her—back down to earth after an experience like this, Lisi gestured nervously towards the teapot.

'Shall I be mother?' she asked brightly.

'You *are* mother,' Philip responded softly. 'Aren't you?'

She sat down and busied herself with pouring the tea. She had gone so long without mixing with men that she was in danger of misinterpreting everything this particular one said.

She glanced up to find him watching her, the beautiful green eyes narrowed thoughtfully. 'Who's babysitting to-night?' she asked.

'It's a surprise.'

'I don't know that I really like surprises—and I think I ought to know, so that I can prepare Tim.'

Philip hesitated. Was he about to break an unwritten law of betraying an official confidence? But it *was* to Lisi, and Lisi he could trust.

He looked over at Tim, but Tim was oblivious to everything, save his exciting new train-set.

'Choo!' he crooned. 'Choo!'

Philip lowered his voice. 'It's Khalim,' he explained.

'Sorry?'

'Khalim,' he repeated.

'P-Prince Khalim?' Lisi gulped in disbelief.

'That's right. And his wife. Rose.'

Who just happened to be a princess! Lisi put the teapot down with a shaking hand. Her son was about to be looked after by the leading members of Maraban's royal family! 'Surely they're not *that* strapped for cash!' she joked, her voice rising with a very faint note of hysteria.

Philip gave her a rueful smile. 'It does tend to have that effect on people,' he admitted. 'Everyone was a bit taken aback when they first knew he was joining us at Cambridge—but only for a time. When you are young, these things seem to matter less. *Some* people liked him for all the wrong reasons, of course—but Khalim is adept at picking out falsehood. He is a consummate judge of character, despite the isolation his position inevitably brings.'

'What will I say to them?' moaned Lisi.

Philip smiled. 'Say what you would say to anyone. Just be yourself.'

Lisi handed him his tea and gave him a puzzled look. 'I can't understand why they want to spend their Saturday evening babysitting for someone else?'

Philip took the tea and gave her a noncommittal smile. There were some confidences which were not in his gift to break. 'Normality is what they crave above all else,' he said blandly. 'Somewhere where they can relax, and be themselves.'

After tea he showed Tim his room. It had obviously been decorated especially in his honour. There were bright walls and framed posters of cartoons and more toys.

'You're spoiling him,' protested Lisi weakly.

He shrugged. 'I have a lot of time to make up for.'

She walked quickly over to the window, his remark reminding her that he would never forget the secret she had kept from him all those years. But would he ever forgive her?

'Come on,' he said. 'I'll show you where you're sleeping. Next door to Tim—of course.'

It was surprisingly small and cosy, with a fire burning brightly in the grate.

'I know how much you like fires.' He smiled. 'And this is the only bedroom in house which has a fire, apart from mine, of course.'

Her heart gave a skip of disappointment. Of course he wasn't going to move her into *his* bedroom—why on earth should he, when the physical attraction between them had obviously died? For him, at least. But, oh, she knew one mad, wild moment of longing as she pictured herself in his arms, and in his bed.

'Shall I start to get dressed now?' she asked, with a glance at her watch. 'What time are they getting here?'

'Seven-thirty,' he said.

'I'll make sure I'm ready on time.' She smiled. 'Don't worry, Philip—I won't keep them waiting.'

He smiled back. Very astute of her to realise that, despite the fact that Khalim and Rose were as close to him as they were to anyone outside their family—the fact remained that they *were* different. Only a fool would keep them waiting and Lisi was no fool. 'I'll leave you to it.'

She showered, made her face up, blow-dried her hair and pinned it back with tiny, diamanté clips, but she couldn't do the damned zip of her dress up!

She sighed, knowing there was nothing else for it but to ask Philip—and there was absolutely no reason to be shy when he knew her body more intimately than any other man.

Nevertheless, she could feel her cheeks pinkening as she called along the corridor.

'Philip! Can you zip me up?'

Philip paused in the act of clipping on his cuff-links and grimaced. Yes, he *could* zip her up, but was there any worse torture for a man who had vowed not to lay another finger on her until the time was right?

'Philip?'

'Coming,' he replied, silently cursing himself for his poor choice of word.

She stood outside the door of her room, and shrugged her shoulders apologetically, trying desperately to distract herself from the magnificent sight he made in formal dinner clothes which set off his lean physique to perfection. 'I'm afraid that I have to be almost shoe-horned into it!' she babbled.

Shoe-horned? All he could think of was how stunning she looked in black, the stark colour setting off the paleness of her skin to perfection and reflecting the deep ebony of her hair.

She turned around so that her bare back was facing him, and he sucked in a raw breath to see that she was not wearing a bra, and that her magnificent breasts were to be held in place only by the clinging folds of heavy silk.

He caught hold of the zip as gingerly as if it had been a poisonous snake. He could feel the warmth radiating off her skin, and the drift of some sweet, subtle perfume invaded his senses.

The temptation not to close her dress up, but instead to lay his fingertips against the silky surface of her skin was so powerful that he felt the unwanted jerk of arousal. He wanted to lead her by the hand to his bedroom, and to slowly undress her and make love to her all night long, but he knew that he could not. And not just because Tim was up and awake.

Time seemed to have stood still, and Lisi felt the waves of longing as they washed heatedly over her skin. She could hear the very definite sound of his breathing and she wondered whether he was actually going to get round to doing her dress up, even while her body craved for him not to, but to turn her round and kiss her instead.

'How's that?' he ground out, using every atom of self-restraint he possessed as he jerked the zip up.

'Fine! Thanks,' she gulped and fled back into the sanctuary of her room, hating herself for wanting him so badly, but hating him even more for not wanting *her*. What could have happened to kill all his desire for her?

Her impulsive response might have turned him off. That eager and frantic bout of love-making might have prompted him into thinking that it was inappropriate behaviour for the mother of his child to act in such a free and easy way.

When she eventually emerged from her room, she found him waiting for her and thought that she heard a distant barking. 'Do you have a dog?' she asked in surprise.

He shook his head, pleased to be able to focus his mind on something other than how utterly irresistible she looked. 'That'll be Khalim's people.'

'People?'

'Bodyguards,' he explained. 'They'll have dogs patrolling the grounds, as well as a couple of people stationed out front and out back.'

Lisi nodded thoughtfully. 'It must be strange to live your life like that—always being monitored and never alone.'

'They have each other,' said Philip simply. 'Their love makes everything bearable.'

Lucky Rose, thought Lisi, with a painful leap of her heart. What wouldn't she give to have that kind of closeness with Philip?

'Let's take Tim downstairs and feed him, before they arrive,' he suggested, then added, almost as an afterthought, 'You look beautiful, by the way.'

'Thank you.' She gave a weak smile, wishing that he had said it as though he really meant it, rather than just subjecting her to the kind of cool, green gaze as if he had been admiring a particularly expensive piece of furniture.

They gave Tim boiled eggs and toast and then settled him down in one of the big armchairs, happily drinking a glass of milk and watching one of many videos which Philip must have bought specially. Lisi looked at them with interest. He had certainly gone out of his way to make sure that Tim felt at home here. She might hope in vain that he would be openly demonstrative to *her*, but there was no doubting the love and pride he felt for his son.

Khalim and Rose arrived at the appointed hour, and Lisi stood nervously at Philip's side while he introduced them.

'Should I bow or should I curtsy?' she had asked him moments earlier.

'Either will do.'

In the end she managed an odd mixture of the two, but she was more than slightly awestruck by the sight of the black-eyed prince and his exquisite, blonde-haired princess.

'So you are Lisi.' Rose smiled. 'And this must be Tim.'

On cue, Tim jumped excitedly to his feet, not seeming at all phased by his high-born child-minders. He gave a little bow just as Philip had taught him to, and Khalim and Rose both laughed in delight.

'Sweet,' murmured Rose, and a dreamy look came over her face.

'He has your profile, Philip,' said Khalim suddenly, and subjected Lisi to a blinding smile. 'And his mother's magnificent colouring.'

'He has many of his mother's qualities—and not too many of mine, hopefully,' responded Philip.

Lisi found Rose's eyes on her. 'Khalim?'

He turned to his wife immediately. 'Dearest?'

'Bring me some sweet mint tea, would you, my love? And take Philip with you, and Tim. Show them how domesticated you have become!'

The prince gave a rueful smile, looking a little like a tiger who had just been offered a saucer of milk. 'You see how she orders me around, Philip? That much at least has not changed!'

'Indeed,' came Philip's murmured response as he followed Khalim out of the room. It never failed to amuse him—the autocratic leader of Maraban's ruling family capitulating to his English wife's every whim!

Once they had left, Rose beckoned towards the sofa. 'Come and sit by me.'

Lisi waited until Rose was seated and then sat down next to her.

'Philip has told us much about you,' observed Rose softly.

Lisi bit her lip. 'Oh? May I ask what he said?'

'That you were an exemplary mother. And that you were very beautiful.'

Lisi hesitated.

'Do not be afraid to speak,' commanded Rose softly. 'We are not on ceremony here.'

'Did he tell you about…about…'

Rose shook her head. 'He told *me* nothing that you would not wish us to hear, I think—though he is naturally closer to Khalim. Just that the circumstances surrounding Tim's conception were not ideal.'

Which Lisi supposed was a fairly diplomatic way of putting it.

'But my romance with Khalim was not a simple, straight road either,' mused Rose. 'We encountered many rocky paths along the way. This is often the way of love, you know.'

Love, thought Lisi. And although her heart ached with longing, she knew that she could not confide in the princess and tell her that Philip did not love her, nor ever would. To the outside world their relationship might look close, and it was not her place to make the reality known to his friends.

Rose leaned back against one of the cushions and gave another dreamy smile. 'Now, tell me, Lisi,' she said softly. 'Is childbirth really as bad as they say it is?'

Lisi narrowed her eyes, but did not ask the obvious question. 'It's different for everyone,' she said slowly. 'Some women find it easier than others.'

'And you? Was it easy for you?'

Lisi stared into the princess's clear blue eyes. 'It was different for me,' she answered candidly. 'I was all on my own. There was no partner to hold my hand or massage my back, or just to tell me that everything was going to be all right.'

'I will be on my own, too,' sighed Rose and nodded in answer to the silent query in Lisi's eyes. 'Yes, I carry the prince's child. But Khalim will not be permitted to enter the birthing chamber—it is not the Maraban custom for fathers to be present. I will be attended to by his sisters and my ladies-in-waiting, and with that I must be content.'

'I would buy every available book on the subject if I were you,' advised Lisi. 'And practise breathing techniques and relaxation—that can really help.'

Rose nodded, and then she laid her slim hand on Lisi's hand. 'You know that Philip can be very hard on himself, don't you?'

Lisi opened her mouth to ask her what she meant, but the moment was lost when Philip, Khalim and Tim reappeared, carrying the tray of mint tea.

A car arrived to pick them up, and it wasn't until they were speeding towards Hyde Park that Lisi turned towards Philip's shadowed profile.

'Rose is pregnant,' she said. 'Did you know?'

The profile shifted so that he was facing her. 'She told you that?'

Lisi nodded. 'Yes. You sound surprised.'

'I am. I would not normally expect such a personal admission from her, not on such a short acquaintanceship.'

'Actually, I'd kind of guessed.' She saw his eyes narrow. 'It's a woman thing—you can usually tell if another woman is pregnant.'

'Khalim is over the moon,' he observed softly, looking at the soft line of her lips and knowing that later he intended to kiss them. 'They both are.'

Lisi stared out of the window without really seeing anything. If only she could have had Philip's baby within the context of a warm and loving relationship like Rose and Khalim's.

'Why did you invite me tonight, Philip?' she asked suddenly. 'Did somebody let you down at the last minute?'

He swore softly beneath his breath. 'If any question was designed to remind me that you continue to think the worst of me, then that one was. I asked you, Lisi, because I thought it would be a treat for you.'

'The country girl let loose in the Big City?'

He ignored her sarcastic tone. He didn't want to fight. Not tonight. 'I can assure you that tonight you look like the most sophisticated city slicker I've ever seen!'

'Shall I take that as a compliment?'

'You could try. Now stop frowning—you'll grow old before your time. Try smiling—we're here.'

The ball was lavishly spectacular and filled with beautiful people, yet Lisi did not feel out of place—though that probably had something to do with the fact that Philip did not leave her side all night.

He danced with her and introduced her to countless people. He fetched her food and idly fed her titbits with his fingers, and because she didn't want to make a scene she didn't stop him. Didn't want to stop him, if the truth be known.

Just after midnight, the party was still in full fling, and they had just finished dancing a very slow dance in the candlelit ballroom. Lisi was reluctant to move from his arms, and he seemed in no hurry to make her. She sighed, wanting to rest her cheek against his shoulder once more, to breathe in the heady masculine scent of him and to pretend for a while that they were real lovers as well as parents.

'Lisi?'

'Mmm?'

'Look at me—I want to ask you something.'

She glanced up, something in his voice telling her that this was not a perfunctory question about whether she would like another drink. 'Yes, Philip?'

His face was as emotionless as if he were asking her the time. 'Will you share my bed tonight?'

CHAPTER ELEVEN

'MUCH as I adore Khalim and Rose, I thought they'd never go,' whispered Philip as he drew her into his arms, and quietly closed the door of his bedroom behind them.

Part of Lisi had not wanted them to go. All during the drive back from the ball she had been a bag of nerves, sitting bolt upright in the seat and wondering if she had dreamt up his provocative question and her breathless agreement to sleep with him. But this was what she had wanted for much too long, wasn't it?

He had glanced at her set features on the journey home. He certainly hadn't been going to start making love to her there, with the interested eyes of the driver looking on. Not that he'd trusted himself. If he'd started, he couldn't imagine ever wanting or being able to stop, and tonight he wanted to do it properly—with a lazy and unhurried dressing and the comfort of his big bed awaiting them.

'Lisi,' he said softly now. 'Have you changed your mind?'

She shook her head.

'Scared, then?'

She nodded. 'A little apprehensive.'

'Well, don't be. There's nothing to be apprehensive about. Here.' He lifted her fingers to his mouth and slowly kissed them, one by one, and he felt a little of the tension melt away from her. Then he pulled the diamanté clips from her hair and it fell down around her pale shoulders in streams of dark satin.

With wide eyes Lisi stared up at him, and he thought that she looked like a trapped and cornered animal. 'Lisi,' he sighed. 'We don't have to do this, you know. I thought that you wanted it as much as I do.'

Her voice trembled. 'And I do. You know I do. It's just…'

'What?'

'You haven't come near me for weeks, nor shown the slightest inclination to. I thought that you didn't want me, not in that way.' She swallowed. 'So what's happened to change your mind?'

He gazed down at her with a mixture of dismay and disbelief. Not want her? He had never stopped wanting her! Was he really so difficult to read, or just a master at keeping his feelings disguised?

'I've always wanted you, Lisi,' he said quietly. 'But our passion always seems to spring up on us unawares. I didn't want to try to make love to you at your cottage, afraid that Tim might hear because he's next door.'

'He's next door now,' she pointed out.

'And the walls here are decidedly thicker,' he commented drily.

She wasn't going to get offended by that. He was merely stating a fact, not making a comparison between the basic structure of her little cottage and the luxurious proportions of his.

'I want to make love to you properly,' he whispered and began to trace the outline of her trembling mouth with the featherlight brush of his fingertip.

The glitter from his eyes made her glow from within. 'I always quite enjoyed it when you made love to me improperly,' she joked, and he leaned forward and dropped a kiss on her lips.

'That's better,' he murmured approvingly, and her arms went up around his neck and the kiss became extended. '*Much* better. Isn't it?''

'Mmm!' She swayed against him, her doubts banished

by the warmth of his mouth and the expert caress of his tongue.

'Shall I undress you, sweetheart?'

The term of endearment made her shakier than the kiss had, and she nodded, her heart beginning to pound as he slid her zip down and laid bare her breasts.

He bent his head to take each sweet nipple in turn, inciting them into instant life with the lazy flicker of his tongue as he slid the dress down over her hips and it fell with a sigh to the floor.

He looked down at her and sucked in a ragged breath. 'Stockings,' he said thickly. 'You're wearing stockings.'

Yes, she was. 'Y-you said that you liked them,' she said, almost shyly. And tights would have seemed all wrong beneath such a fairy tale of a dress.

He wanted to beg her to keep them on, to make love to him with those silken thighs pressed hard into his back, but he knew that there would be another time for that. Right now he wanted—no, needed—her to be completely naked, there to be nothing between the two of them except skin.

'Shall I take them off for you?' he questioned unsteadily.

'Yes, please.'

His hand was shaking as he unclipped the suspender and then took a deliberately long time sliding the gauzy silk down over every delicious centimetre of her legs, his face moving tantalisingly close to the dark, triangular blur of hair which concealed her most precious gift. He longed to bury his mouth in her most secret place, but resisted, fearing that he would only end up taking her on the floor.

He unhooked the suspender belt and it joined all the other garments on the carpet and then he lifted her up and carried her over to the bed, covering her up with a duvet, so that only her cute nose and those huge aquamarine eyes were showing, and the shiny fan of black hair lay all over his pillow.

He began to unbutton his shirt, never taking his eyes from her face. 'Want me to undress for you?'

Beneath the concealment of the duvet she felt herself melt. 'Y-yes.'

The shirt fluttered from his fingers and he began to undo his trousers. It was hard to reconcile this sweetly shy Lisi with the wild lover who had gripped his shoulders so ecstatically, her fingernails making tiny little nips into his skin, her back pressed up against the wall as he'd driven into her over and over again. He stifled a groan.

Her eyes growing wider by the second, Lisi wondered what had made him briefly close his eyes like that, or why suddenly he seemed to be having more than a little difficulty sliding his zip down.

Arrogantly, he kicked off the trousers and the silk boxers followed and he stood in front of her for a moment, wanting her to see what she did to him. How she could turn him on to this pitch without having laid a finger on him.

He pulled back the duvet and climbed in next to her, and pulled her into his arms, kissing the top of her head and enjoying its meadow-sweet scent. He would just hold her for a while, stop her trembling and make her feel safe.

But the trembling only seemed to get worse, and he pulled away from her, noting the look of acute distress which had creased her brow into a deep frown.

'What's the matter, sweetheart?' And then he saw that her eyes were almost black, they were so dilated. And her breathing was shallow and rapid, and he moved his hand down between her legs to feel her slick, inviting heat. He groaned. He had been planning to make this one last and last—but what the hell? They had all night.

But he had something he needed to tell her, something she deserved to know. 'You remember the last time we did this, that morning at the rectory?' he asked, in a low voice.

'I'm not likely to forget in a hurry.'

'And you told me that there had been no other lover since me?'

She nodded. Had she been mad to expose such obvious vulnerability?

He gazed down into her watchful eyes. 'Well, it was the same for me, Lisi. There had been no one else. No one.'

There was a short, breathless silence and she could have wept with the pleasure of discovering that. 'Oh, Philip,' she murmured, and held him very close.

Lisi lost count of the number of orgasms she had that night; her last reality check was drifting into sleep sometime in the early hours, when dawn was already beginning to bring a pale, clear light to the sky.

He woke her at six and made love to her again, and she knew that she really ought to get up and get out of there before Tim got up, when there was a little rap on the door, and Tim's voice calling.

'Daddy?'

Locked in each other's arms, they both froze and looked at one another, but Lisi knew immediately that there was no way around this without the whole situation being turned into some kind of farce.

She nodded at him and he understood immediately.

'In here,' he called back. 'Come in, Tim.'

Lisi held her breath, expecting shock or outrage or even—perhaps—a touch of early masculine jealousy from the male who had been in her life the longest, but Tim displayed none of these.

Instead, he ran over to the bed, carrying his night-time bunny, glanced over at the two of them and said happily, 'Oh, *good*! Now you're just like *Simon's* mummy and daddy!'

And Lisi didn't know whether to laugh or cry.

'Why don't you go downstairs and do me a drawing?' suggested Philip. 'And I'll come down in a minute and get you some juice while I'm making Mummy her morning coffee.'

'But Mummy has *tea* in the morning.' Tim pouted.

Philip nodded. 'Then I'll make her tea,' he said gravely.

'Okay!'

They heard him scampering down the stairs and their eyes met.

'That was easier than I had anticipated,' admitted Philip.

'You were expecting him to find us in bed, then, were you?'

He shrugged. 'Well, it had to happen some time, didn't it?'

How *sure* of himself he was—and how sure of *her*. But she wasn't going to be a hypocrite and feel badly about the most wonderful night of her life.

He gave her a quick kiss, and yawned. 'At least this makes things easier.'

Lisi stilled. 'How do you mean?'

'Well.' He paused and lifted her chin so that she could not escape the cool scrutiny of his eyes. 'How would it sound if I told you that I was moving to Langley?'

The words did not seem to make any sense. 'I don't understand.'

'I love the rectory,' he said softly. 'And I find myself increasingly frustrated at commuting down there every damned weekend, when I'd happily see Tim every day.'

Tim. Not her. Just Tim. 'Go on,' she said painfully.

'So I've decided to base myself in the village.'

'But what about your business?'

He smoothed a lock of hair away from her cheek, noticing that she shut her eyes very quickly. 'Technology has given people in my kind of work the freedom to work from anywhere.' He hesitated, drawing back from telling her the one really *big* bit of news.

She opened her eyes, sensing that something else was coming. 'What?' she questioned.

'I'm in the process of buying Marian Reece out.'

'You're *what*?'

'Don't look like that, Lisi.' He put his hand on her shoulder, but she shook it away and sat up in bed, her hair tumbling down to her waist, and he had to stifle the urge to start making love to her again. Tim was downstairs, he reminded himself, though he could see from the angry look on her face that an attempt at love-making *now* would not be particularly well received.

'You just didn't bother telling *me* that you're about to become my new boss?' she accused crossly. 'And neither, for that matter, did Marian!'

'It was tricky for her. She was undecided about whether or not she wanted to stay or go—she'd been thinking of it for some time, apparently.'

'But presumably you made her an offer she couldn't refuse?' she asked sarcastically.

'I gave her a good price, yes, but then I wanted—no, I *needed* a property base in Langley.'

'Perhaps you'll be pushing the existing staff out, and bringing in new people altogether!' she said, her voice rising on a note of hysteria. 'Or maybe I'll just hand my notice in—that might be best all round! Have you thought what it would be like if we were working together?'

He had thought of little else. 'I'm not going to make you do anything you don't want to, Lisi,' he said placatingly. 'I wasn't planning to be hands-on—particularly as I hoped we might be spending a lot more time together anyway.'

She stared at him uncomprehendingly. 'Because you'll be seeing more of Tim if you're living in the village, you mean?'

'Well, not just Tim. You, as well—that's if you agree to my next proposal.'

Proposal? Her hands had gone suddenly clammy. 'Your proposal being what, exactly?'

The words had gone round and round in his head count-less times, but there was no guaranteed way of making sure that she would not take them the wrong way.

'I thought that you and Tim could come and live with me. At the rectory.'

Her heart stood still. *'What?'*

'It seems crazy for us to live in two houses on the same road, when the three of us seem to have forged a pretty good relationship.'

Pretty good relationship. How tepid and passionless that sounded!

'And last night proved something, didn't it?'

'What?' she asked shakily.

'That you and I are compatible in many, many ways.'

He meant, of course, that they were good in bed together. She guessed that it was intended as a compliment, so why did it make her feel distinctly uncomfortable?

Because sex without love was only ever second-best, that was why.

She wondered whether last night's magnificent seduction had all been part of his grand plan. Have her begging in his arms for more and she would not be able to deny him anything.

Least of all his son.

She supposed that she could toss her head back in a gesture of pride and thank him for his charming 'proposal', but tell him that she preferred what she already had.

But it would be a lie.

She had already decided that she couldn't bear for any-one else to have him and that she would settle for whatever he was offering. Hearts and flowers it was not, but perhaps it was the best she could hope for.

'What do you say, Lisi?' he asked softly. 'Will you and Tim come and live with me?'

She tried telling herself that for Tim's sake she could not refuse, but that would not be the whole picture. For her sake too, there was only one answer she could possibly give.

'Yes, Philip,' she answered quietly. 'We'll come and live with you.'

CHAPTER TWELVE

'No, Mummy!'

'But, darling, you *need* a new pair of shoes—you know you do—and we're going to meet Philip's parents at the weekend. They have to see you looking your best, don't they?'

'Granny and Grandpa,' said Tim happily.

Lisi suppressed a sigh. Everything seemed to have happened so quickly. It seemed bizarre that a few short months ago it had been just her and Tim, and yet now he talked all the time about Daddy, and his grandparents and the uncle and aunt he was soon to meet.

One great big extended family—for him, at least—although Lisi still sometimes felt as though she was standing looking in from the sidelines. But her role was as Tim's mother and Philip's mistress, and she must never forget that.

The move from Cherry Tree Cottage to The Old Rectory had been seamless—practically, if not emotionally. She had been apprehensive about it at first, but her fears had been groundless and it had turned out to be nothing short of a delight to move into her old home, with all its happy childhood memories.

To the outside world they probably looked just like any other family—and, indeed, that was just how it felt most of the time. In every sense of the word.

After years of abstinence, Philip certainly wasn't holding back. He made love to her at every opportunity he got, and Lisi wasn't complaining. He took her to heaven and back every time, even if the words of love she longed for never materialised.

He was warm and tender when she lay in his arms, but he didn't let his defences down—nor she hers. He never told her whether he regretted that circumstances had forced them into this quasi-marriage, and she didn't dare ask. And he, like her, seemed happy enough to go along with the status quo. Either that, or he was a consummate actor.

He had persuaded Marian to stay on in a consultant capacity. She now worked mornings only, two new staff had been taken on, business was booming—and Lisi had been promoted to office manageress in the afternoons.

'Philip, I can't!' she had protested, when he had first mooted the idea. 'Everyone will say it's nepotism!'

'Then everyone will be wrong,' he had replied patiently. 'You've worked here for years, and you've worked damned hard. You're good—you know you are! You deserve it, Lisi—so enjoy it!'

And she did—especially so on the all-too-infrequent occasions when Philip himself was in the office. He had not exaggerated when he had told her that he did not plan to be too hands-on. He continued to travel around the countryside and, as often as not, chose to work from the beautiful study he had created at The Old Rectory, where he said the view made his heart sing, and Lisi had never thought she could be so jealous of a view!

Thank heavens she was essentially a practical person, determinedly enjoying what she had and not wishing for the impossible.

But the trip to meet his parents loomed. She wanted to make a good impression, and that meant a brand-new outfit as well as shoes for Tim.

'Let's leave Daddy a note, shall we?' she suggested. 'You can do him a little drawing while I load up the dishwasher before we go. Here.' She scribbled a few words down, resisting the desire to add hundreds of kisses. 'Have taken Tim to Bilchester to buy shoes and a dress for me—back in time for work. Love, Lisi.'

Tim grizzled from the moment she put him in the car, and Lisi wondered whether he was coming down with a cold.

'Don't *want* to go!' he screamed, and she looked at him.

Which was more important—a happy son, or a miserable son? His trainers weren't *that* bad—and surely Philip's parents would be more interested in seeing their grandson, than in analysing her choice of footwear for him! She glanced at the heavy clouds in the sky, and the thought of being caught in rain with an out-of-sorts Tim made her mind up for her.

'Tell you what,' she said as the car Philip had insisted on buying her bumped its way down the drive. 'We'll call in to see if Rachel's there. If she is and if she isn't too busy, we'll see if you can stay with her and Blaine, while Mummy goes to Bilchester on her own. How does that sound?'

'Hurrah!' cheered Tim.

Rachel seemed all too pleased to have him. 'That'll keep Blaine from under my feet.' She grinned. 'I have four tons of laundry to sort out, and all he wants to do is play!'

Bilchester was quiet, but Lisi suspected that the drizzle which had now turned into a torrential downpour had something to do with the lack of shoppers.

She managed to buy a flame-coloured dress and a sexy pair of suede shoes, but her umbrella did little to withstand the gathering gale, and by the time she got back in the car she was shivering.

Her progress back was slow and she found herself looking at her watch more than once, and she was just starting to get anxious when she felt the car pulling out of control, and she managed to steer it over to the side-verge before switching off the engine.

With the rain pouring down, she got out to investigate and her worst fears were confirmed when she looked down to see that her tyre was completely flat. To drive it would be madness, but how the hell did she get home?

She looked up and down the narrow lane, as if expecting a recovery vehicle to come roaring up to her aid, but the road was completely empty and she was miles from anywhere.

So did she sit in the car and wait, and hope to flag down a passing motorist who might just turn out to be a homicidal maniac?

Or should she start walking home—or at least to the nearest phone-box? Philip would be home and he could drive out and pick her up.

Her raincoat already almost soaked through, she took her bags and set off as icy mud spattered up the sides of her legs and the heavens continued to unleash their downpour.

It took for ever to find a phone-box, and by then she felt that there was not one part of her body which wasn't cold and wet.

With chattering teeth she inserted a coin and dialled home, but the phone rang and rang and she remembered with a sinking heart that she had not put the answering machine on before she had left.

She replaced the receiver with a sigh of resignation. Nothing else for it but to carry on walking.

Never had a journey seemed quite so long or so arduous. Two cars passed her, but she let them drive on by—she was nearly into Langley now. A little way more wouldn't kill her.

It was almost two o'clock when she trudged past the duck pond and down the lane towards The Old Rectory. With frozen fingers she was fumbling around in her bag

for her doorkey when the door flew open and there stood
Philip, his face so white and furious that she hardly recognised him.

'Where the hell have you been?' he exploded, although
the frantic racing of his heart abated slightly.

She was taken aback by the dark fury in his eyes. 'Well,
that's a nice way to greet someone,' she managed, but her
teeth were chattering so much that her words sounded like
gobbledygook.

'I've been worried sick! Worried out of my head! You
left a note saying that you'd gone out with Tim and I
thought...I thought...' he heaved in a shuddering breath
'...I thought that something had happened to you!'

Lisi pushed past him into the hall, suddenly understanding his distress. He was out of his mind with worry, but it
had been Tim who had been the cause of his concern, not
her. Of course it had.

'Why do you have to be so damned stubborn?' he demanded. 'Why wouldn't you let me buy you a mobile
phone?'

'Because I don't need one! I've never had one before
now, and I'm not going to start now just because I have
the good fortune to be living with a rich man!'

'How charmingly you put it!' he snarled.

'Well, it's the truth!' She had never seen Philip quite so
het-up before. Never. She glared at him. 'Why haven't you
even bothered to ask me where Tim is, as you're so worried
about him?'

'I know where he is!' he snapped. 'He's at nursery! I've
just taken him there. Rachel rang here to find out where
you were because you hadn't collected him, and I told her
that I didn't know. You didn't ring—'

'Yes, I did! There was no reply—'

'I was out collecting Tim, that's why. Did you bother to
put the answering machine on this morning?'

'Did *you*?' she countered. 'Anyway, there's nothing to worry about now, is there? Tim's safe, and that's all that matters!'

'All that *matters*?' he said incredulously.

'Yes!' she snapped.

He went very still, and his face took on an implacable look she had never seen there before. 'Take that coat off,' he said suddenly. 'You're soaking.'

She attempted to undo her coat, but her fingers were shaking so much that they slipped ineffectually at the buttons and Philip reached across to help her. She tried to swat him away. 'G-go away!'

He ignored her. 'Now go and get changed,' he ordered. 'And then come down to my study. I've lit a fire.'

She had had enough. Too tired and cold and shaken to care about what she said, she shot him a look of defiance. 'Stop sounding like a bloody headmaster!'

'Then stop behaving like a naughty schoolgirl!'

His rage was both intimidating and yet oddly exciting. 'And if I don't come down?'

He gave a grim smile as he slipped the sopping coat from her shoulders. 'Don't stretch my patience, Lisi—I've taken just about as much as I can stand from you this morning.'

There was something about his stance and his attitude which made all the rebellion die on her lips. Of course he had been worried—wouldn't she have been out of her mind herself in the same situation?

She changed into jeans and a big, thick sweater and towel-dried her hair, and when she walked into his study, not only did he have a glorious fire blazing, but he had also made tea, and a large bowl of soup sat steaming on the tray.

He handed her the soup. 'Eat that,' he commanded.

There was something so unimpeachable about the expression on his face that Lisi took the bowl from him obediently and began to drink it, while he stood over her making sure she did.

When she had finished the soup and drunk some tea, and the colour was beginning to seep back into her pale cheeks, he sat down in the chair opposite hers beside the fire.

Lisi pouted. The least he could have done was to have taken her upstairs and to have brought complete warmth back into her body by making love to her.

Philip saw the way her eyes darkened and the way her lips had softened. He knew what she wanted, but she was damned well going to have to wait! For too long now, he realised, he had allowed the intimacy of the bedroom to help shield him from confronting *real* intimacy.

'Did you really think that it was only Tim I was concerned about?' he demanded. 'Didn't it enter your pretty little head that I might be worried sick about *you*?'

She met the accusatory green glitter of his eyes. So he wanted the truth, did he? Then the truth he would have. 'Not really, no.'

'Lisi.' His voice was incredulous. 'Why on earth do you think that you're here, living with me the way we have been? Why do you think I asked you to move in?'

'Because that way you can have Tim full-time, and a sex life into the bargain!'

He stared at her. 'You honestly think that?'

'What else am I to think? You've never told me anything apart from the fact that I'm a great mother and a great lover. Oh, and a great cook.'

'And that isn't enough?'

She wasn't going to ask him for anything he couldn't offer freely. 'It's obviously enough for you.'

There was a moment of fraught silence. 'Oh, but it isn't,' he said softly. 'Not nearly enough.' This kind of thing didn't come easy to him, but he was going to have to try.

'You see, what I want more than anything else is your love, Lisi.'

She stared at him. 'Why?'

She needed to ask him *why*? He shook his head impatiently. Didn't she *know*? 'Because I'm finding that I can't hold back my love for you. Not for much longer. I love you, Lisi—hadn't you begun to even guess?'

She didn't respond for a moment. When you had spent so long wishing that something would happen, you didn't believe the sound of your own ears when it seemed as though something just had. 'You don't have to say things like that to make me feel better.'

'I'm not,' he said patiently. 'But what if saying them makes *me* feel better? What if I told you that I don't know when I started loving you, but I do, and not just because you're mother and lover and cook, but because you make me laugh and you make me mad, and I can't imagine the world without you. And the only unknown factor in this equation is that I don't know how you feel about me.'

She felt hope—delirious, impossible hope—begin to beat out a rapid thunder in her heart. 'You must do,' she said weakly.

'Why must I? You never tell me what's going on inside your head, do you, Lisi? At night you never whisper anything more tender than the fact that I'm a bit of a stud in the bedroom.'

'And what about you?' she countered. 'You're the master of disguising your feelings! If, as you say, you love me— then why didn't you tell me before? Why didn't you make that a part of asking me to move in here with you, instead of leaving me feeling like a mistress-cum-mother?'

'Is that what I made you feel like?'

She nodded.

He sighed. 'Because I didn't know how much I loved you until you became a part of my life,' he admitted. 'It kind of crept up on me slowly, like a sunny day at the end of winter.'

Curled up in her chair, Lisi felt some of the tension begin to leave her. 'Something still stopped you, though, even when you realised?'

'I was scared,' he said simply.

'Scared?' Lisi smiled. 'Oh, no! That really *would* be stretching credibility too far—I can't imagine you being scared of *anything*, Philip.'

'Scared that it would all sound too pat. That you wouldn't believe me—and why should you? I thought you would begin to see for yourself, only…'

'Only what?' she prompted, her heart in her mouth.

He shook his head as he read the doubts and fears in her eyes. 'It was like you had erected a barrier between us, and sometimes you would lower it down, but only so far—so I didn't have a clue whether you knew how I felt. Or how you felt about me,' he finished, a question in his eyes.

He had been about as honest as it was possible to be, and she knew that, to Philip, such admissions did not come easily. It was time to make her own.

'I was scared, too,' she whispered. 'Only my fear was that the love I felt for you might frighten you away. Falling in love wasn't supposed to be part of the deal, even if that's what I wanted more than anything.'

A slow smile began to transform his face into the most carefree Philip she had ever seen. 'Come here,' he whispered.

She didn't need asking twice, just went and sat on his lap, and he wrapped his arms tightly around her waist while her head fell onto his shoulder and she fought to keep the stupid and irrational tears away.

'Don't cry, Lisi,' he soothed as he felt her tremble. 'There's nothing cry about. Not any more.'

She thought about how far she had come to reach this

moment, and, despite his words, the tears spilled over onto his sweater and soaked right through it.

He didn't say another word, just held her very, very tight until a last little sniff told him that she was all cried out, and he lifted her head and gave her the kind of tender smile she had always dreamed of. 'Better?'

'Mmm.'

'Need a hanky?'

She bit her lip and actually giggled. 'I used your sweater, thanks.'

He smiled as he brushed a last stray tear away. 'You once asked me whether that first night had just been lust,' he said softly. 'And I said that I didn't know.' He paused. 'That wasn't quite true.'

She stilled. 'What do you mean?'

It was time at last to make sense of all his vague suspicions. 'I talked to Khalim about it—I told him the whole story, and he said that such uncharacteristic behaviour on my part meant far more than I perhaps realised.' He smiled as he touched her lips, just for the hell of it. 'I told you that Khalim was a romantic, but he would prefer to describe himself as a realist. He said that I was being too hard on myself and that my subconscious was telling me that you were—or could be—very important to me. How right he was.' He kissed her tenderly. 'How right he was!'

'Oh, Philip!' She snuggled even closer to him.

'And one more thing.' He kissed her again. 'I'm sick of not letting the world know how I feel about you. I want to marry you, Lisi—just as soon as you like, *if* you like.'

'Mmm! I can't think of anything I'd like better!' She kissed him back. But not for a while. She wanted to enjoy what she had never had with Philip—a loving courtship with no pressures.

'But let's take it step by step,' she whispered. 'Better get your parents used to having a grandson before we announce that you're getting married!'

His mouth trailed a lazy line down her cheek and he felt her shiver. 'Nervous about meeting them?' he questioned.

'A little.' She pressed herself closer, revelling in the knowledge that there were no secrets or taboo between them now. Love, she realised, was a very liberating emotion. 'We've done everything the wrong way round, Philip.' She sighed. 'Haven't we?'

'It certainly hasn't been a text-book love-affair,' he agreed. 'And I need to take you to bed,' he added softly.

She felt the raw need and tension in his body, but there was one other thing she needed to say to him. 'You must never forget Carla,' she whispered. 'I don't want you to. Let all the guilt go now and remember all good times—she would want that for you, having loved you. I would.'

There was a moment of silence. 'That's about the sweetest thing you could have said,' he said shakily, and right then he needed her as he had never needed her before. He gave a slow smile. 'We'll have to go and collect Tim in an hour, you know.'

'I know. And?'

A finger was grazed carelessly around the outline of her lips. 'Any idea how you'd best like to fill the time?'

She felt the invasive tug of desire and gave him a bewitching smile, loving the predatory and possessive darkening of his eyes. 'One or two,' she said demurely.

'Me, too. Let's say we swop notes. Upstairs,' he purred, lifting her up into his arms and slanting a provocative smile down at her.

She opened her eyes very wide. 'You're going to *carry* me to bed?'

'That depends.'

'On what?'

'On whether we make it to the bedroom!'

EPILOGUE

SOMEONE was banging a spoon against an empty wineglass and the excited chatter of the guests began to die away.

It had been the most wonderful wedding imaginable. Lisi stole a glance at her new husband and let out a small sigh of contentment. She almost didn't want it to end, except that the night ahead beckoned her with such erotic promise.

Philip slowly turned his head, as though he had known she was watching him, and mouthed 'I love you' with an expression on his face which made her heart feel like spilling over with happiness.

'May I just say a few words?' The banger of the spoon was Philip's father, who was now rising to his feet.

Charles Caprice was a poppet, thought Lisi fondly. Tall and distinguished, his hair brushed with silver, he had given her a very pleasing insight into how her darling Philip would look when he was older.

Philip's mother had been equally welcoming—embracing her as if she were the daughter she had never had, and both of them were absolutely besotted by their grandson. In fact, Tim was going to stay with them while they were away in Maraban for their honeymoon.

She looked around the room. Langley had never seen a wedding like it—but maybe that wasn't so surprising. When a small English village was invaded by the leading members of the Maraban royal family and their entourage, then excitement was pretty much guaranteed!

Prince Khalim had stood as Philip's best man, and an ecstatic Rose had proudly carried the infant Prince Aziz, who had lain contentedly in her arms throughout the ceremony.

'I do not know why Rose has brought along a nanny,' Khalim had remarked drily to Philip. 'She guards him so jealously—like a tiger!'

'And would you have it any other way?' Philip had smiled.

'Never!'

Philip looked down at the jet-dark hair of the baby Aziz, and ruffled it. He had never seen his own son as a baby, and Lisi had cried and cried about denying him that right on more than one occasion, but he had urged her to let it go, as he now had. 'There'll be more babies,' he had whispered.

'Wh-when?' she had questioned shakily.

'Whenever you like. I think Tim would like a brother or a sister, don't you?'

And she had nodded and then kissed him, too full of emotion to speak for a moment or two.

Philip's father was now clearing his throat. 'I know that it isn't conventional for the *groom's* father to speak,' he began, and then sent Lisi a gentle smile across the table. 'But Lisi has become like a daughter to my wife and I— actually, she *is* our daughter, as well as my son's wife. And that's really what I want to say to you all.' His voice faltered a little. 'I would like you all to raise your glasses in a toast. To Lisi, beautiful, sweet Lisi—who has put a smile on my son's face again, and for which I will always be grateful.'

Champagne glasses were lifted and waved in the direction of the top table, but Lisi was so choked that she didn't dare look up for fear that everyone would see her eyes brimming over with tears.

'To Lisi!' they all echoed.

Beneath the table, Philip squeezed her hand. 'Look at me, my darling,' he urged softly.

She lifted her face to his, seeing the corresponding glitter of his own eyes and immediately understanding why. His father's emotional words had reinforced that a bright, new future lay ahead and that the past was now behind them. And in a way, Philip had been saying goodbye to Carla, she guessed, and squeezed his hand back, very tightly.

'It's okay to cry at weddings, you know, sweetheart,' he whispered.

She wobbled him a smile. 'But my mascara will run!'

He laughed. She was everything to him—his passion and his soul mate—the woman who had brought the light back into his life. 'I love you very much, Mrs Caprice,' he told her simply, because he did.

Modern Romance™
...seduction and
passion guaranteed

Tender Romance™
...love affairs that
last a lifetime

Sensual Romance™
...sassy, sexy and
seductive

Blaze-
...sultry days and
steamy nights

Medical Romance™
...medical drama on
the pulse

Historical Romance™
...rich, vivid and
passionate

29 new titles every month.

*With all kinds of Romance for
every kind of mood...*

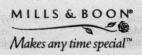

MILLS & BOON®

Makes any time special™

MAT4

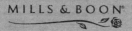

Treat yourself this Mother's Day to the ultimate indulgence

3 brand new romance novels and a box of chocolates

= *only £7.99*

Available from 18th January

2 FREE

books and a surprise gift!

We would like to take this opportunity to thank you for reading this Mills & Boon® book by offering you the chance to take TWO more specially selected titles from the Modern Romance™ series absolutely FREE! We're also making this offer to introduce you to the benefits of the Reader Service™—

> ★ FREE home delivery
> ★ FREE gifts and competitions
> ★ FREE monthly Newsletter
> ★ Exclusive Reader Service discount
> ★ Books available before they're in the shops

Accepting these FREE books and gift places you under no obligation to buy, you may cancel at any time, even after receiving your free shipment. Simply complete your details below and return the entire page to the address below. *You don't even need a stamp!*

YES! Please send me 2 free Modern Romance books and a surprise gift. I understand that unless you hear from me, I will receive 4 superb new titles every month for just £2.49 each, postage and packing free. I am under no obligation to purchase any books and may cancel my subscription at any time. The free books and gift will be mine to keep in any case.

P2ZEA

Ms/Mrs/Miss/Mr ....Initials......................................
BLOCK CAPITALS PLEASE

Surname ....

Address ....

....

....Postcode...............................

Send this whole page to:
UK: FREEPOST CN81, Croydon, CR9 3WZ
EIRE: PO Box 4546, Kilcock, County Kildare (stamp required)